The Dull Dead

"At first I thought, just as everyone did, that Minny had been frightened by someone pestering her in some nasty sort of way and that we must watch over her. And then the more I thought about it the odder it seemed. Minny wouldn't say anything, you see, that was what puzzled me. Because she can talk, Superintendent, she's five, she could have said a lot more. And then I thought, Mrs. Daft put this into my head, that the reason she wouldn't say anything was because she knew the person who had frightened her."

Sergeant Coffin pushed a chair forward just in time; Isobel swayed and sat down in it limply. But she was still talking.

"Heaven knows that was horrible enough. And then it struck me that whether Minny knew who she was talking about or not, she could have said more than she did. I could see that she was frightened and wanted our help, but she wasn't telling all she knew.

"It came to me then that in a horrible sort of way Minny was co-operating."

Other titles in the Walker British Mystery Series

Peter Alding • MURDER IS SUSPECTED
Peter Alding • RANSOM TOWN
Jeffrey Ashford • SLOW DOWN THE WORLD
Jeffrey Ashford • THREE LAYERS OF GUILT
Pierre Audemars • NOW DEAD IS ANY MAN
Marion Babson • DANGEROUS TO KNOW
Marion Babson • THE LORD MAYOR OF DEATH
Brian Ball • MONTENEGRIN GOLD
Josephine Bell • A QUESTION OF INHERITANCE
Josephine Bell • TREACHERY IN TYPE
Josephine Bell • VICTIM
W. J. Burley • DEATH IN WILLOW PATTERN
W. J. Burley • TO KILL A CAT
Desmond Cory • THE NIGHT HAWK
Desmond Cory • UNDERTOW
John Creasey • THE BARON AND THE UNFINISHED PORTRAIT
John Creasey • HELP FROM THE BARON
John Creasey • THE TOFF AND THE FALLEN ANGELS
John Creasey • TRAP THE BARON
June Drummond • FUNERAL URN
June Drummond • SLOWLY THE POISON
William Haggard • THE NOTCH ON THE KNIFE
William Haggard • THE POISON PEOPLE
William Haggard • TOO MANY ENEMIES
William Haggard • VISA TO LIMBO
William Haggard • YESTERDAY'S ENEMY
Simon Harvester • MOSCOW ROAD
Simon Harvester • ZION ROAD
J. G. Jeffreys • SUICIDE MOST FOUL
J. G. Jeffreys • A WICKED WAY TO DIE
J. G. Jeffreys • THE WILFUL LADY
Elizabeth Lemarchand • CHANGE FOR THE WORSE
Elizabeth Lemarchand • STEP IN THE DARK
Elizabeth Lemarchand • SUDDENLY WHILE GARDENING
Elizabeth Lemarchand • UNHAPPY RETURNS
Laurie Mantell • A MURDER OR THREE
John Sladek • BLACK AURA
John Sladek • INVISIBLE GREEN

GWENDOLINE BUTLER
The Dull Dead

WALKER AND COMPANY · NEW YORK

Copyright © 1958 by Gwendoline Butler

All rights reserved. No part of this book may be reproduced or transmitted in any form or by any means, electric or mechanical, including photocopying, recording, or by any information storage and retrieval system, without permission in writing from the Publisher.

All the characters and events portrayed in this story are fictitious.

First published in the United States of America in 1962 by the Walker Publishing Company, Inc.

This paperback edition first published in 1985.

ISBN: 0-8027-3108-2

Library of Congress Catalog Card Numoer: 61-6951

Printed in the United States of America

10 9 8 7 6 5 4 3 2 1

CHAPTER ONE

THE AFFAIR BEGAN in the smallest possible way with the refusal of little Minny Duveen to go to school alone.

She looked frightened and obstinate. But it was difficult to get much information out of her.

"Man," she said.

The whole household gathered round her.

"What man?" asked her father.

"Man," said Minny again, after a pause.

It was a very small beginning to all the misery and horror to follow, but there was menace enough in it.

"Imagination," said her father uneasily.

"She hasn't got any imagination," said Mrs. Duveen dryly. "None of the children have."

She did not add 'they take after you', but her husband could supply this for himself. One way and another he had been trained to read between the lines in social relations. Not for nothing was he an extremely successful barrister who might one day be a judge. He had spent the war years looking after a bevy of neurotic Guardsmen (Major S.D.B. had been his rank), who were more or less ready to do or die but who were also desperately anxious to reason why. In the process of helping them he had learnt a good deal about human nature, but, unfortunately, he sometimes thought, not enough.

He looked out of the window. The Duveen house in Pontifex Passage overlooked a little square of London park which in turn looked down upon the river. The family was in the drawing-room; it was the nicest room in the house and Isobel had composed it as carefully as one of the pictures she used to paint. The walls were white and no little hands had finger-printed them and this was due to the adamantine severity with which Isobel kept the girls out of the room. Window curtains of a surprisingly deep and vivid green framed the windows and on the wall by the door was their most valuable picture, a little Sisley. From the big bay window there was a distant view of the river and of Lambeth Bridge. "Sweet Thames run softly," thought Robert a little sadly. His Thames never did run softly.

He was puzzled by his wife. She was taking this business of Minny oddly.

Isobel Duveen was the mother of four girls and she was a woman who would have made a better mother of boys. Her girls irritated and charmed her; she thought them pretty, all except Minny who was plain, poor love, and silly. She regarded the silliness as a legacy from her own mother, Lady Passey. This lady had been a very Bright Young Thing, had adored Noel Coward and Michael Arlen and had called her eldest, and as it turned out, only child, after lovely unlucky Iris March. Iris Isobel had dropped the Iris as soon as possible, *her* particular literary gods being Hemingway and Auden.

Isobel Duveen was a lovely, irritable figure, much placated by her family (all except Lady Passey), who felt that one way and another they were not what she had hoped for. The remark about imagination was typical of her.

"Oh, Mummy, that's simply not true," protested Perdita the eldest girl. "I've got loads of imagination."

"You're different," said Isobel with a shade of irony.

Perdita digested this, her pretty full lips pouting, but her big blue eyes looked at her mother quite sharply.

"I don't like it," said Isobel. "What *has* happened to upset her? I could have sworn she's not been anything but normal every day, and now, suddenly, *this*."

"Children bottle things up."

His wife gave him a weary look. "Some things. Some children. Your grasp doesn't go deep enough."

"Well, she isn't giving us much to go on, is she?" asked her father irritably.

"If it's going to school that she's frightened of," said her mother slowly, "then there must be something in that. She's only alone for the last two hundred yards, a walk along a little row of houses with the park on the other side. The others are with her right up till then. In the space between the entrance to the school where the other two go and Minny's kindergarten there's something that frightened her."

"Well we know what," said Perdita. "Man."

Minny gave her a quick look.

"I wish Minny would speak up," said her father.

Perdita appraised Minny. "You won't get any more out of her. After all she's only five."

She looked at her two other sisters, the twins aged nine, who were watching silently. They had big brown eyes like Minny but Perdita's eyes were like her mother's, a bright deep blue.

"We don't know anything," they said regretfully. "Tell you if we did."

"You're going the wrong way about it," said a voice from the door.

A small plump figure stood there with arms folded.

"Hallo, Mrs. Daft," said Robert in a pleased voice. Isobel looked resigned.

Mrs. Daft was a figure well known in all the four houses that made up the short road of Pontifex Passage. Every day she crossed the river from South London in a bus to work for Isobel Duveen and her neighbours the scatty old gentleman at No. 3 (known as the Mad Hatter), the youngish ambitious politician at No. 4 and the group of three young professional men at No. 5 (known to Mrs. Daft as 'my boys') on whom her heart was really set. She was a willing but not naturally methodical soul and her well-meaning attempts at cleaning added considerably to the confusion of all four establishments. Isobel kept her because she was a friend of the Duveens' Scandinavian cook who had to be humoured at all costs.

Now she stood there in her stiff, starched and none too clean overall and looked at them severely.

"You're going about it the wrong way." She rustled over and put her arm round Minny's waist.

"Have you been spoke to, love?"

Minny considered. "Spoke," she said at last.

Perdita swung her leg. "I don't know how you feel but I don't seem to hear much conviction in Minny's voice."

"Put your legs in a more seemly position do, Miss Perdita," said Mrs. Daft, who was unexpectedly prudish in many ways. Her little face with its untidy and rather grubby knot of hair was grim.

"Spoke?" she said, in a questioning tone to Minny.

There was a moment's silence. Minny presumably had no more to say.

"She had a tube ticket in her pocket last week," said one of the twins suddenly in a high voice.

None of the children travelled to school by tube, and as far as was known none of them ever went in a tube at all. Isobel drove them everywhere in her little green Austin.

"Well, there it is," said Mrs. Daft, rising to her feet with a creaking. (Poor old Daft and her rheumatism, thought Perdita.) "Now you know. Someone's been getting at the little love."

She looked solemn.

"You'll have to make up your mind where to look. Is it inside Pontifex Passage or not?"

Robert Duveen went to the window. The September sun had fallen behind the trees but the air was filled with a lovely green glow. Far away over the roof tops came the melancholy wail of a ship on the river.

"We've got the whole of London to look in," he said.

He turned to face his family. Unconsciously he took up the position he used when cross-examining hostile witnesses.

"There must be something that one of you knows."

The Duveen family, although they had nothing to say to each other, had their confidences to make: Robert Duveen doubtfully and sceptically told the police; Isobel told her lover, by letter, for he was away;

and Perdita told Tom, her current young man who was training to be an architect.

Perdita and Tom were walking in the little park. The sun shone on their bare heads and made them gleam with gold. They were both fair and tall but Tom had an air of nervous strength which was lacking in Perdita, who was really quite placid, although Mrs. Daft said still waters run deep.

They were accompanied by the twins and Minny and a few hangers-on who had somehow attached themselves.

"We'll have to shake some of this lot off," said Tom with a despairing glance at a little boy with an ice-cream cone and a girl with a toffee apple. "Are you going to have to bring your sisters everywhere?"

"I expect so. Mummy's quite worked up."

"Mind you, they're nice children." He took Minny's hand. "All the same . . ."

"It's all Mrs. Daft's fault really," said Perdita with a sigh. "If Mummy slackens off for a bit she reminds her. You know what people like that are."

"I know what Mrs. Daft is like," said Tom who was one of her 'boys' at No. 5 Pontifex Passage. "What a name, poor old bird, eh?"

Mrs. Daft was quite proud of her name really, she thought it a mark of distinction. Perdita had asked her once how she had come to actually marry someone called Daft.

"Me name's Daft he said to me when he asked me to marry him. Oh, well, there's many dafter I says. And it wasn't as if I was leaving such a good name of my own behind, my dear," she said with a grin to

Perdita. "Blood it was and that lays a girl open to a lot of jokes if her dad's a butcher."

"A butcher was he, Mrs. Daft?"

"Well, not to say own the shop, dear. I don't want to boast. In fact I doubt if the old dad ever owned anything."

"Anyway, you took Mr. Daft?"

"I did, my dear. Daft by name but not by nature I said to him kindly." She paused. "Though as to that I'm not so sure as things turned out later. Poor old Daft. Still he was a good man. I don't say anything of him as a husband but he was a good man. Share his last penny with a stranger. When he had one, that is, which wasn't often what with the drink and the dogs."

Perdita giggled as she remembered this, then she remembered that giggling was unsophisticated now and not in keeping with a young woman who had had one season as a débutante and had a part-time job with a very chic photographer.

"What with your social whirl and your job and your nursemaid duties I never see you now," complained Tom.

"Not so much of a whirl these days," said Perdita. "Only one party this week. People are beginning to despair of me, you see, I nearly always have to take one of the children or rush off to collect them. It's beginning to get me down. Of course it's September so everyone who counts is in Scotland or Venice but still . . ."

In the distance they could see flames leaping in a bonfire and a park-keeper silhouetted against the blaze as he fed the fire with leaves and rubbish.

"Lovely smell," sniffed Perdita. "Oh, I do love autumn. Let's go and see the fire, come on, Minny. Twins, stop fighting and walk." She gave them a friendly push.

The park-keeper nodded as they came up. He knew Perdita and Tom by sight, and he now knew Minny by reputation.

"See you've got the little girl with you."

"Yes," said Perdita surprised; she had not understood that other people outside the family knew about Minny and their worry.

"Oh, I know about it, of course. The police always notify us in the parks. Obvious when you come to think of it. I keep a look-out anyway."

"You do?"

"Oh, you'd be surprised. We gets lots of characters hanging round the kids in the park. I chase 'em off."

"And I always thought the park was a nice quiet place," said Tom.

"Oh, we see life in the rough here all right." And the park-keeper leaned back against his broom and closed his eyes. Tom saw that he was asleep standing up.

"Damn it, he's like a horse."

"We'd better go back," said Perdita uneasily. "It's nearly time for tea and the park doesn't seem quite so nice as it did." She gripped Minny's hand tightly. "Just supposing if someone was watching us now."

"Miles away," said Tom with a lightness he did not feel, "if Minny was not making it all up."

"I don't think she was," said Perdita, "and Mrs. Daft thinks——"

"Don't tell me what she thinks. Let's feed the birds."

He held out a crumb of bread and at once a swarm of angry and grubby sparrows appeared. A large and aggressive bird made a swift grab at him. Tom drew back his hand hurriedly.

"Damn it," he said grimly. "Even the birds in this place would peck your eyes out."

The young constable going sedately down Pontifex Passage looked back and saw Tom and Perdita and the little girls going into the house. He paced on, hands behind his back and a look of solemn contemplation on his face. He passed No. 2 (there was not and never had been a No. 1) where the Duveens lived; No. 3 where old Mr. Booth lived. "I'd like to know more about *him*," said the constable, nodding to himself. He caught sight of Mr. Booth's bald head with an aged bowler resting on it. Mr. Booth nodded at him cheerfully, he seemed to be eating something. Behind Mr. Booth and his bowler the constable could just see the empty and deserted, although clean, room. Mr. Booth waved a sandwich. "Mad as a hatter really," said the constable to himself and laughed at his joke.

No. 4 Pontifex Passage was still closed up he noticed. Still away on that trade mission, of course, the papers had been full of it. He nodded sagely to himself. He had his own ideas about No. 4. Well, politics was a tricky business. And he had seen Mr. Cobley coming out of those offices in Leadenhall Street. Not that there was anything not respectable about the offices, on the contrary they were highly respectable, the headquarters of a firm of bankers, and that was precisely what was so odd.

The constable (he was a young man from Kent called John Evelyn) turned on his heel and looked back to where he could see into the little area of dusty green grass that was the Duveens' garden (Isobel planted it with geraniums in summer and asters in winter but they never thrived). No one was in the garden but Minny Duveen and she was solemnly watering a patch of bare earth with water from a long-spouted green can.

He looked at her thoughtfully. He knew about the trouble over Minny. He had been present when the Divisional Inspector and Sergeant had discussed Robert Duveen's visit. Pontifex Passage was only a stone's throw from divisional headquarters and this had angered the sergeant.

"Right on our doorstep," he said. "Nerve, you know."

"Yes, but what?" The inspector in his way too was angry. "It's all so intangible. A child is frightened but can't say of what, or where, or why. Nothing we could put our finger on. Nothing we can do. Except wait. And watch." He was a man with children of his own and he was alarmed and anxious. "Watch for what? We shan't know until the trouble hits us."

As Minny turned over her little plot of earth and the constable watched her a memory stirred uneasily within him. He rubbed his chin thoughtfully.

He went on his way past the last house of all in Pontifex Passage, No. 5, where lived the three young men so liked by Mrs. Daft. It presented a rakish appearance in a sedate road. The three occupants had a floor each, one room really because it was a narrow little house, and each had their own ideas, or lack of them, about decorations. Tom who lived on the ground floor had bright chintz curtains supplied by his mother, they were not pretty but were, as she put it, wearable, and 'would not show the London dirt' which in view of Mrs. Daft's activities was perhaps desirable. Berry (if he had another name no one knew it) lived above Tom and had had his curtains supplied by his girl friend, a lovely and languorous model. She had provided him with curtains of imitation bamboo,—'very smart'—which looked exactly like hanks of string. These, too, did not show the dirt which made them a success. On the top floor behind dark green curtains lived Jack O'Finney, the young doctor; his curtains were filthy as he had lived in the house three years now and had bought the curtains from the previous inhabitant, but Jack being a doctor and anyway not home much was impervious to dirt.

Jack O'Finney and Berry were sitting drinking beer in the top room behind Jack's green curtains. Presently Tom, drawn up by the noise, abandoned his work and went up to them.

"Hallo, boy," said Berry. "Saw you out with all the little girls." He stuttered a little.

"Oh well..."

"No need to be embarrassed, boy, Perdita's a pretty little thing."

"Not so little," said Jack in a professional sort of way. "Five feet eight and still growing."

"Oh, I hope not," said Tom in alarm.

"Don't take any notice of him," said Berry. "How'd you get on today, Jack? Pull through?"

Jack scowled. "No damn it, dead again," he said, throwing himself into a chair and taking up a paper.

"Who is?" asked Tom nervously.

"It's his operation," said Berry sympathetically. "Very important. But they never survive."

"Nuisance," growled Jack.

"Yes it must be," said Tom even more nervously. "Especially for them."

"Oh, well," said Jack, cheering up as he took some more beer, "I'll just have to keep at it. More tomorrow."

"You're going to keep at it?" Tom was awestruck. He was thinking of *them*.

"Oh, rather. Why not? Scientific research you know."

"It does seem hard though that they should all die. Still I suppose they're sick to begin with."

"Oh, good lord, no, I always choose healthy ones. Naturally. And I will say this for the little perishers, they fight for their lives."

Tom went white. "But don't the relations mind? And isn't there an inquest?"

Jack stared at him and laughed. Berry leaned forward.

"These are rats, boy, not people."

Tom cheered up and drank some beer. But all the same he was sorry for the rats. Jack, he thought, although no doubt a good doctor was a tough nut and not overflowing with gentleness of spirit.

"I've heard about the Duveens' trouble," said Berry. "Nasty. Nothing in it, perhaps."

"Well, I think there is," said Tom looking down into

his beer. "Perdita's worried and she says that Mrs. Daft says——"

Jack coughed loudly.

"Hallo, dears," said a voice from the door. "Just come in for me evening tidy up. Needs it by the look of it. You choking, doctor?"

"Oh, no, Mrs. Daft, only swallowed some beer, have some?"

"Not till I've done my work," said Mrs. Daft virtuously, as she made mopping motions with a grubby duster. She was not efficient but she was willing and she would turn her hand to anything from cooking a great and rather nasty shepherd's pie to a bit of valeting. "Your hair needs cutting, doctor. Like me to have a go?"

"No, thanks," said Jack quickly. "And the family?"

"Well," said Mrs. Daft, "as well as they're likely to be." She sighed.

If Mrs. Daft was a willing worker she expected in return that her young men should run a sort of advice bureau. She used Jack for medical advice and was often seen having muttered conversations about symptoms; she used Berry for all matters of finance on the grounds that he worked in a bank (although Berry was slightly indignant at having his very grand bank compared unfavourably with the Post Office and the local Friendly Society) and Tom got the residue of her worries on the grounds that they were all connected with her house and he knew about houses, didn't he? As a result the lives of the three young men were peopled with phantoms from Mrs. Daft's life and they knew all about her daughter and the new baby and all about Dad Daft and his bad eyesight. They were never quite sure whether he was dead or not, sometimes his wife spoke as if he was dead and sometimes as if he were alive.

"Oh, Mr. Tom, I wanted to ask you, my drains are smelling something terrible, what should I do?"

"Oh, lord, I don't know. Put something down them I should think."

"Something *is* down them," said Mrs. Daft. "That's what I'm complaining about."

"If she knew how little I knew about houses," said Tom gloomily, "she wouldn't ask me. I never do anything but check specifications, estimates and blue prints. Do you think I'll ever be a proper architect? But then again it's such a responsibility. Sometimes I'm haunted by the thought that a house or a theatre I'd built might fall down. I never realised before that I was tampering with other people's lives."

"You get that too in medicine."

"You certainly do. Berry's lucky here, just dealing with money."

"We had an old man in today," said Jack sombrely. "It fell to me to give him some bad news about himself. He took it badly. Oh, well, it's the sort of thing you must expect, you get 'em all in hospital, deaths that shouldn't happen, and births that shouldn't either. It's all right if you can keep it impersonal."

"I suppose you can."

"Oh, yes, usually, but in a hospital like this, serving a small area with a heavy concentration of population, one does sometimes know the patients."

Tom thought about this. "Yes, I can see your point. Imagine having Mrs. Daft turn up!"

"Yes," then Jack grinned. "Well, I'm glad to say that so far I have escaped Mrs. Daft in person." He drank some more beer and looked critically around him. For the first time it struck Tom that he had been drinking for some time.

"Another one of your flashy ties, Berry, I see."

"It was a present."

"Yes, I couldn't imagine even *you* going and buying it. Oh, well, I know that being a present makes it sacred. I've had that sort of present myself." He squinted at it. "And believe it or not it was just that sort of pattern. Same girl no doubt. Watch out Berry, dear, if it's the same girl. A vicious little piece in some ways."

"Oh, I say," said Tom jumping up. "Be careful, chaps, you'll break something."

He had noticed before, and with alarm, that there was a natural turn for violence in Jack, and that it was quick to waken an echo in Berry.

"This isn't a prep school," said Jack to Tom. "Get out of the way, little 'un."

But it was Jack who twisted backwards across the room, Berry who rubbed his arm in pain, and Tom who stood quietly, but breathing quickly, between them.

"Sorry," he said. "Painful I know. I hate that sort of dodge really but you two were getting rough."

"A little trick you picked up in the army I suppose," said Berry. "You just about broke my arm."

"It's all knack," said Tom absently.

"You'll kill each other one of these days," said Mrs. Daft, threading her way unperturbed between them.

"Well, ta ta, I'm off to see the old boy next door, poor old duck, he gets madder every day."

As she went off Jack remembered something. "What is it you were going to tell us about Mrs. Daft?"

"Oh, yes," said Tom. "Well, it's her idea about this business with Minny?"

"The father I suppose? She thinks one of the criminal classes that he's put away has got round to working his grudge out on Minny?"

"Robert Duveen never comes near a criminal. He's a Chancery Lawyer. No..."

"I dare say he might have irritated someone, a judge say or a solicitor. I know he irritates me."

"That's not Mrs. Daft's idea," said Tom.

"Well, what is her idea?"

"Go on, boy," said Berry.

"Well, the thing is she thinks it's one of us," said Tom simply.

CHAPTER TWO

FOR A WHOLE week from Monday to Monday Isobel drove the twins and Minny to school in her little Austin. This activity interfered, as her husband had half suspected, with certain plans of her own, for the process worked both ways—if she was keeping an eye on the children, equally they were keeping an eye on *her*. Perdita also found her life disturbed by the need to watch over the children but she was in a position to complain loudly about it.

"I'm not only thinking of parties, mother, I'm thinking of my *work*!"

"How virtuous of you, darling."

"Poldy doesn't like it. And you can't blame him. He never knows when I'm going to dash off to meet the children from school or dancing class or those ghastly friends of theirs." Poldy was her employer, a highly temperamental Roumanian photographer with a large and fashionable clientele just about balancing his overdraft. "He's always worse on a Monday because Sunday depresses him so. And then, Mother, I had to go round to Madame Lanca's to try on the hat she's making for me. *Had* to, Mother, and Minny came too. She had four hats out and was wearing them one on top of the other before I could stop her. Didn't please Madame."

"Poor Minny," said her mother. "And *such* hats."

"Well, that's a matter of opinion, Mother. Personally I think she's bliss. But what is certain is that the twins have no manners. Little roughs."

"Yes, perhaps they are a little."

"The way they talk to people," grumbled Perdita. "No idea. You for instance, now why can't they call you mama instead of mum, so much prettier, and perhaps give you a little curtsey."

"Oh, my dear, no," said Isobel. "*Too* café society. You have *no* taste. Just like your father."

This stone was aimed at two birds, Perdita, who did not like to be told she had no taste, and her husband because he was not, and sadly regretted it, Perdita's father.

"Anyway, tomorrow you'll have to get Mrs. Daft to collect them from dancing class. I can't because as a matter of fact I shall be modelling." A look of pride spread over Perdita's face.

"I hope he pays you this time," observed her mother. "Such a disappointment last time when he didn't." There was usually an edge on the remarks between the two.

"Don't forget to see Mrs. Daft gets the children," was all Perdita said.

"But Tuesday is her day for next door," said Mrs. Duveen. "You know very well that on Tuesday she takes Mr. Booth next door to the hospital, they spend the whole day there."

"Hell," said Perdita. "She won't give *that* up. It's her big day. Personally I think the old boy ought to be put away. Well, I ask you, he is crackers, living in that bare house and imagining it still full of beautiful furniture."

"He's not mad, poor thing," said Isobel sadly. "Only unhappy."

"Well, I hope unhappiness never gets me that way."

"No, darling, it won't," said Isobel, even more sadly. "You're one of the rush out and do things sort."

"Well, *don't* say ' Just like my father!'"

Isobel was silent.

"Anyway, you've got to admit he enjoys his day at the hospital and so does Mrs. Daft, she picks up enough gossip to last her through the next week. Oh, good evening, Mrs. Daft. How are you?"

Mrs. Daft made quite an entrance. She was dressed in her best blacks and even Perdita and the absent-minded Isobel knew the significance of this splendid appearance.

"What is it, Mrs. Daft?" asked Perdita gaily. "A wedding or a funeral?"

Smoothing the feather on her best hat Mrs. Daft bustled forward to collect the tea-tray. She knocked over a cup so that a little tea dribbled out on to the tray. She rubbed at it cheerfully with a duster she had tucked under her arm. Not for the first time Isobel wondered where Mrs. Daft had received her domestic training, if any.

"Won't leave a stain, me dear. When I get down to the kitchen I'll drop a bit of salt on. Karen's busy that's why I come in for the tray. You wouldn't be expecting me and I'm not here by rights, only visiting as a friend, you might say. It's a lovely dinner Karen's cooking you for tonight. Chicken à la something or the other and a souffley. I'd have come in and waited if you'd asked. I've been practising. I dare say I wouldn't drop anything this time."

"It's kind of you, Mrs. Daft, but it's only a small dinner party, and I can see you've got something planned yourself this evening."

"Well, I have, and it's not a funeral or a wedding, miss." She turned to survey her old enemy Perdita. "My friends don't get buried or married after tea, wouldn't be right. I've got to pay a call," she said. "Just business."

Mrs. Daft's business, although supposed by her to be a deep secret, was in fact well known to all her employers. She ran a little subscription club for Christmas. Isobel thought that no one subscribed to it, or hardly anyone, but that Mrs. Daft enjoyed the round of visits it entailed. As it was now September business would be hotting up. Probably tonight Mrs. Daft was going to buy the goods for which members would be subscribing. That nice woollen dress as advertised in the catalogue (Isobel herself had once been approached in a discreet sort of way to join) or the plastic crocodile handbag.

"Well, right you are," said Mrs. Daft. "But if I was you, I'd call the little girls out of the kitchen. Karen says they're getting in her way. Their sister could play with them, glad to I expect," she added with a look at Perdita.

Isobel hurried to the door. It would never do to have Karen put off her cooking on the day when Judge Mosse and her mother Lady Passey were both coming to dinner. Although her mother had long since got over her marriage to Robert and even enjoyed his company still she was apt to be difficult. "Of course, I do see dear that with Robert you've got to be tactful but couldn't you get him into a livelier branch of the law where he could meet a few criminals and make a name for himself? After all, all those patents and contracts and so on, not very gay is it? I've nothing against lawyers, far from it, they get to be very distinguished, look at Lord Simon, but you've got to keep at them. And get a good cook dear even if you have to go without a new fur coat, it's really not fair to your friends or husband if you don't." "Not fair to me was what she really meant," thought Isobel, knowing that in her oldish age her mother had become quite a connoisseur of food and wine. But then she had never had to give up having a new fur coat either. That was one thing about having a fairly rapid turnover in husbands, you were apt to get a good many presents and perquisites such as mink coats, emerald ear-rings and Dior dresses. Hanging on to a wedding-ring (even if by the skin of your teeth, although Isobel pushed this last reflection quickly to the back of her mind) seemed to make for dowdiness.

"Children, come here quickly," she called down the stairs. She looked regretfully at the peace of her white drawing-room, soon to be invaded by the twins. However when she saw Minny's white little face her worries came rushing back again.

"Come and sit on my lap, Minny dear, and get warm by the fire. Why haven't you taken your coat off?"

She looked accusingly at Perdita.

"Wouldn't," said Perdita briefly answering the unspoken comment.

The twins, who had taken off their coats, bounced about on the pale brocade of Isobel's long lovely sofa in their muddy wellington boots. Even on dry sunny days the twins' round healthy bodies could be counted upon to pick up mud and dirt and scatter it on everything. They could see that their mother was preoccupied and took advantage of this to amuse themselves in otherwise forbidden ways.

"Young devils," said Mrs. Daft passing with the tea-tray. She preferred Minny although she admired the twins.

"I suppose you couldn't meet them tomorrow instead of me?" asked Perdita hopefully.

"Got to take me old dear to the hospital," said Mrs. Daft cheerfully. "Oh, I know what you're thinking, but it's no treat to me to take the poor old fellow, I can tell you. They don't seem to get him better, nor will they ever I'm thinking. Bring him back next week they say and we'll have a look at his back, or his teeth, or his stomach, or wherever they can think of next—as if all that'll bring his poor old memory back. He don't remember because he don't want to. I tell 'em that but they take no notice any more than they did when old Daft was going. It's no good I said to them, he's made up his mind to go and he *will* be gone. But that's doctors all over, knocking themselves over to save someone who don't want to be saved and then letting a life slip through their hands that ought to be saved." She pushed the twins off the sofa where they had now installed the big tabby cat too. "How's the little 'un, Mrs. Duveen?"

Isobel was staring down at Minny. From the pocket of Minny's little blue coat she had drawn out a child's handkerchief. It was small, with a duck embroidered in one corner. It was streaked with a dull red, as if it had been soaked in blood and then, inefficiently, washed out in water.

"Oh, my God," said Mrs. Daft. "How did she get that?"

With shaking hands Isobel was stripping the clothes from a protesting Minny.

"She may be hurt. Where did the blood come from? Minny, Minny, tell me what's happened."

Minny scared and confused, burst into tears.

"Perdita go and get the doctor."

"I'll get Jack," said Perdita preparing to run.

"Oh, my God, no," said Mrs. Daft. "Why it may be *him*."

When Perdita came back a long time later she was accompanied by her father.

Isobel was hugging Minny wrapped up in a blanket.

"Minny's all right," she said with relief. "Nothing wrong with her. The blood must have been some animal or something. Old Tibby perhaps."

Robert took Minny from her mother and handed her gently to Perdita. "Take her up to her room, Perdita."

He sat down gently by his wife and took her hand.

"Not Tibby, darling, but someone has been injured. I'm afraid it's Jack. He's dead, Isobel. When Perdita went over she found him in his room, he'd been dead some time. It looks as though someone killed him."

Isobel began to shake in his arms.

"Don't cry, my dear. I don't say he wasn't worth it because in many ways he was a very worth-while person, but he wasn't worth what you put into it. I've seen you two. Did you think you could hide it from me, Isobel?"

Then he realised that mingled with Isobel's sobs was laughter.

CHAPTER THREE

WHEN SUPERINTENDENT WILLIAM WINTER was directed to investigate the case which started with Minny Duveen he delivered a judgement.

"In cases of this sort concerning a child," he said, "there's one thing to remember." He paused, in his way he was quite an actor. "Always notice the *mother*."

Winter was a thin, rather sad-looking figure whose spectacled eyes belied both his sharp observation and tongue. He had great success in the past as the tough unraveller of murder cases but no success seemed to warm the milk of human kindness in him and he remained a dour figure. It was rumoured that he was going to be married, to a woman he had met in a case at Bow-on-Sea, and it was certainly true he went down to the south coast whenever he was free and that he wore a flower in his button-hole, but no other signs of his betrothal were visible to the anxious eyes of his subordinates. He was no better loved, however, in police and criminal circles where he was known, and not in affection, as the Old Man. He had a new assistant these days. His old helper in cases in London, Sergeant Llywelyn, had been advanced to be an Inspector and to his pleasure did not see Winter so often. His new assistant was Sergeant Coffin, a tall, dark, dapper man much given to calling people dear. If he had not been a policeman he would have made a very good barrow boy, he was agile, clever, quick tongued and unscrupulous. "How did he get into the police force?" Winter asked fiercely on one occasion. "How did we ever come to let him in?"

"I don't suppose he called the interviewing committee dear," said Llywelyn. He got some amusement at the clash between the two.

Winter had arrived in Pontifex Passage within an hour of the discovery of Jack O'Finney's body.

Jack dead seemed a very much smaller person than Jack alive and full of roaring energy. He lay on the floor of his room, in a bright peacock blue dressing-gown and scarlet suède slippers. He had had his hair cut and made some attempt to tidy up the room so perhaps he had been expecting a visitor. Someone had struck him deep vicious blows on the side and back of his head. There were bruises on his cheeks and on his chin. And his hands were torn and bruised. The police doctor said he had been dead for about eight to ten hours as far as could be judged.

"And he died in a fight?" said Winter, forming a rapid judgement and passing it on in the form of a question to the police surgeon.

"Looks like it. But you can't ever tell, can you? I'll be much surer after I've had a good look at him."

"I say, Superintendent, dear," said Sergeant Coffin. "The boy had some lovely clothes didn't he?" He was fingering the silk dressing-gown.

"Just like a spiv," thought Winter observing him irritably. "Rich, I suppose," was all he said. "What was he?"

The police doctor turned from his rapid inspection of Jack's bookshelves.

"Same trade as me. He was going to specialise in obstetrics and gynæ, judging by the books but he hadn't got there yet. Not old enough. Clever fellow."

"You knew him?"

"No, but I can tell by the books he's read and I haven't," said the police surgeon dryly. "Besides he must be clever to be doing his post-graduate work at St. Clare's. They only take the cream."

"How do you know?" asked Winter.

The doctor pointed to an envelope on the shelf addressed to J. O. O'Finney, St. Clare's Hospital, S.W. "Don't let me do your work for you."

He went to the door. "Good-bye, dear," he said to Coffin, getting his dear in first. "Good-bye, Winter, let me have the body by the morning."

Whatever kind of woman Winter had imagined Mrs. Duveen to be, plump, homely, the mother of four girls, the picture he had of her cannot have been what he expected. He had not expected to be ushered in to a tall, fair, pretty woman in a long black gown, pouring sherry.

Isobel, seeing his surprised look, jumped, for once, to the wrong conclusion.

"It is rather late for sherry I know, but what with one thing and another, well, we *are* late."

Frivolous, thought Winter tightening his lips. He was sharp enough, however, to notice the signs of tears beneath the powder and eyeshadow. He could feel Coffin at his elbow and hear him breathing heavily down his neck.

"We were going to have a dinner party," said Isobel stumbling on in explanations she was aware should not be given. Nerves always went to her tongue. Putting off the dinner party had itself been an ordeal. "We were having my mother and some—visitors," she ended lamely for even Isobel flinched at saying we were having a judge and his wife to dinner and we didn't think we could quite ask them to meet the police, not if we have Robert's career in mind. "As a matter of fact once you've seen them I shall be sending the children to my mother."

"Oh, no, *not* Granny," said Perdita sitting down heavily. Perdita had changed for dinner in her own way also, and was wearing candy-striped trousers and a loose shirt made of black velvet. She looked very pretty and heart-rendingly like her mother. "She's so old fashioned."

And so a grandmother should be was written all over Superintendent Winter's face.

"Oh, I grant you she has lovely clothes and she's kept her figure (the four husbands had something to do with that I suppose), but it's her *mind*. She's got stuck in the Noel Coward and the early Evelyn Waugh period. She keeps asking me if my friends drug and how often I get drunk."

"What a grandmother," thought the scandalised Winter. "Like mother, like daughter," he added to himself.

"Why, of course we don't get drunk," said Perdita. "How could we afford to? Why I've only been to one party since I came back from France in August and there was nothing but hock cup at that."

"Austerity," said her father.

"Of course, I'm not saying anything about what the older people do," said Perdita virtuously.

"And look at them all," thought Winter, "all dolled up."

"I suppose you think we ought to be in black or something," said Perdita, reading his thoughts with appalling accuracy. "Well, actually Mother is, and this thing of mine has a black top you see, and it's very old. And I liked old Jack." Tears formed in her eyes. She sniffed just as one of the twins might have done. "He was kind to old Tibby when he cut his paw and I liked him even if he was a bit of a brute and frightful with women."

In spite of herself she looked through her tears to see what effect she was getting.

"And what do you know about that?" asked her father.

"Oh, everyone knows," said Perdita.

"Do they indeed?"

"Well, you did for one."

Winter looked at the group of three people so busily making trouble for themselves.

"Yes, you must have done. I heard you say so to him once 'Quite a Don Giovanni, aren't you, Mr. O'Finney,' you said. Well that only means one thing, doesn't it?"

"Yes, but that—what I meant was," Robert turned to face what he recognised as his true audience. With dignity he said, "I meant his voice, Superintendent. *Don Giovanni* as my uneducated daughter apparently forgets is the name of an opera by Mozart. You need a fine voice to sing the main part, and Jack O'Finney had one."

"Dear me, Mr. Duveen," said Winter falsely, "I wasn't thinking anything else you know." He looked at them jovially. "I'm a police officer not a crook." He turned round to see Sergeant Coffin absently stroking the head of a valuable Bow shepherdess. Perdita was gazing at him in delight.

Winter turned to Isobel who was still standing holding a decanter of sherry. Outside the door Karen could be heard banging around with plates and dishes. Her soufflé had been ruined and she was taking out her temper on Isobel's Crown Derby.

"It's really you I came to see, Mrs. Duveen. I understand there's been some trouble with the little girl."

"Yes, Minny," said Isobel hesitating. "Well I suppose you know all there is to know. It started about a week ago, just over perhaps, she was frightened, wouldn't go to school by herself, even though it's such a little distance. We thought someone had been pestering her, a man, she said. I don't know. And now this? What has this got to do with Minny?"

"It may have nothing at all to do with it, Mrs. Duveen. We can't tell yet. But I think I'll have to get you to give me the handkerchief you found in her pocket. We'll need it you see."

Isobel looked round helplessly. "It's about somewhere I suppose. Perdita, did you take it?"

Perdita shook her head.

"And you weren't home were you, Robert? Well it must be *somewhere*."

She started to turn over cushions in a puzzled and muddled way. Robert looked at her puzzled alarm. It was unlike Isobel, even taking all that had happened into account, to be so very——

"Never mind that now, Mrs. Duveen. To tell you the truth I think it will turn up and if it doesn't perhaps it isn't so important. But I am afraid what I shall have to do to all of you here is to ask you some questions about where you have been today and when. I must be able to rule out as many people as possible you see, because we are afraid this poor lad was murdered."

"I don't see how we can possibly be connected with it all," said Robert promptly.

"I'm afraid you are connected all the same."

Isobel moved uncomfortably. Winter was aware of a deep unease in her beyond even the worry natural over what had been happening to Minny. By training and instinct he probed at this unease.

"It's been a worrying business over the little girl. It was a week ago you first became aware of all this?"

"Yes, about that. Yes a week ago Minny wouldn't go to school alone."

"But the other little girls were all right?"

"Apparently."

"That's odd, isn't it?"

"No, not really. There is a space of a few yards where Minny is alone."

"But it worried you all the same?"

"Oh, well, of course. You can see why. We didn't know what *had* happened and we didn't know what might happen."

"So what did you do?"

"You ought to know that." Isobel was beginning to protest under what she recognised as pressure. "The children were always accompanied to school or wherever they went."

"Who did this chiefly?"

"I did, or Mrs. Daft, or Perdita."

Winter frowned. "You felt they were responsible enough?"

"I'm perfectly responsible," said Perdita angrily.

Isobel, who was still clutching the decanter, turned very white.

"I don't see the drive of some of your questions, Superintendent. This business with Minny, ghastly and worrying as it was, seemed to me, part of a pretty common pattern."

The superintendent expressed the conviction that had been gathering in him.

"Mrs. Duveen, I have had, unhappily enough, considerable experience with the sort of worry you have had with your daughter and it seems to me to fit by no means into the usual pattern of sex crimes."

Robert tried to interrupt but Winter stopped him.

"I think Mrs. Duveen has known for some time, perhaps from the very beginning, that the worry about her daughter was not what it seemed."

Isobel put the decanter down very carefully.

"No, no, that's not quite true. At first I thought, just as everyone did, that Minny had been frightened by someone pestering her in some nasty sort of way and that we must watch over her. And then the more I thought about it the odder it seemed. Minny wouldn't say anything, you see, that was what puzzled me. Because she can talk, Superintendent, she's five, she could have said a lot more. And then I thought, Mrs. Daft put this into my head, that the reason she wouldn't say anything was because she *knew* the person who had frightened her."

Sergeant Coffin pushed a chair forward just in time; Isobel swayed and sat down in it limply. But she was still talking.

"Heaven knows that was horrible enough. And then

it struck me that whether Minny knew who she was talking about or not, she could have said more than she did. I could see that she was frightened and wanted our help, but she wasn't telling all she knew.

"It came to me then that in a horrible sort of way Minny was *co-operating*."

Isobel moved quietly down the stairs and out of the house. The superintendent had gone, Robert was shut into his study, having refused to talk to anyone, and Perdita was reading the children to sleep, reading to them endlessly from *The Wind in the Willows*, droning on and on.

Judging by the smell, Karen was making coffee in the kitchen, and judging by the rattle of voices she had Mrs. Daft there with her.

Isobel was quite sure no one heard her go. Pontifex Passage was near to a Tube station and down its welcome hole Isobel descended. In fact she had a young plain clothes constable behind her but as she did not know this she was unworried. She caught the Charing Cross line and changed twice for Chancery Lane.

It was not late and there were still plenty of people about. She had a dark cloth coat over her black evening silk and no one noticed her particularly, but all the same Isobel was glad that there was an unobtrusive side entrance to her destination.

A wave of warm stuffy air from a building which had never been aired since it had been built three centuries ago, swept into her face.

"A church," thought Isobel. "What a place to meet." She could picture well what her mother would say if she ever heard of it, surprise, amusement and a certain amount of scorn would certainly figure loudly in the reaction of one who had never had reason, or seen it anyway, to hide her love affairs.

Isobel could see, however, that such a meeting place, tucked away off Fleet Street, suited Christopher in many ways. It represented, of course, only an emergency site, even Isobel drew the line at the use of the back pews for more than conversation. And their relationship had notably not been one of conversation only, although that had certainly played its part, too great a part perhaps. It was to be wondered what the Rector and the parish council of St. Mellitus would have made of the whole episode.

"Why a church?" said Isobel with irritation as the long black curtain which hung by the door wrapped its dusty folds around her. Was it, after all, beyond the bounds of possibility that they should meet openly and casually like ordinary people in restaurants, hotels or parks? Why this hunt through hole and corner? Did it in fact so greatly serve either Robert's career, which she was supposed to be considering, or Christopher's which he certainly was? Probably they were both the sort of people who like drama for its own sake. "So I'm like my mother after all," thought Isobel wryly.

"The thing, I suppose," she said to Christopher as she found him and sat down next to him, "is that Robert is not amusing."

"And I am?"

"Unfortunately, you are. In that way, yes. And I'm afraid it was something I'd got used to."

"Yes, I can see that once married to the person you

had been married to it would be difficult to see the joke of dear Robert. Not that I'm criticising him. That's something we've never done I'm glad to say."

"Well, we're not really in a position to, are we?"

"But, Isobel, my dear, why did you get me here? Not to tell me that Robert is not your kind of a joke?"

"I'm glad you came though."

"Yes, it was good of me, especially as strictly speaking I'm not supposed to be in the country at all."

Quickly and quietly Isobel told him. "And not only is Jack dead but Robert supposes me in love with him."

"It's a nuisance," he said.

"Well, a bit more than that I'm afraid." This was, she knew, just his politician's trick of understatement when it suited him and not heartlessness.

"I'll have to try and keep out of it, Bel, I'm afraid."

"Yes, I can see that. And naturally it's what *I* prefer too."

"Not one for burning your bridges are you?"

She sighed. "The trouble is, you see, that they are always other people's bridges, too. We've had this out before."

"You do see, don't you, that *you* are in this business, and so inevitably, am I?"

There was a little bustle of noise and movement at the other end of the church. The church was well if dimly lighted and they could see that a meeting of some sort was breaking up. About half a dozen people came down the centre aisle. They were talking together as if they were continuing in a discussion only just broken off. They had come from the vestry.

"The idea is a very good one," said a quick, high voice.

"His ideas are always good."

"It's the *execution* . . . I know for a fact he spent hours arranging the tree. The fact that the lights fused and Father Christmas got a shock every time he touched the tree was not his fault, but . . ."

"The subsidence of the tree, its actually falling over, was certainly his fault."

"We can lay at his door the fact that the presents were unsuitable for children. A gun for a boy is a bad example."

"They liked it though," said another voice heard for the first time.

As the group passed Isobel and Christopher sitting quietly in their seats, some hard, long and critical glances were passed. Christopher returned them. Well behind the group of complainers came a stout figure dressed in black with a clerical collar: he was jangling a bunch of keys, although nothing in St. Mellitus was ever locked up. Christopher grinned. "I'm afraid that we, people like us, represent one of *his* worst mistakes."

When the last person, with much fussing and noise, had bustled out, he turned again to Isobel.

"But, Isobel, you keep saying, in this funny way, that Minny was co-operating." He repeated it, "Co-operating. In what sense can a child of five co-operate, and in what?"

"Helping, aiding, assisting," said Isobel almost wildly. "But in what? If only I knew. But there is an even more horrible thing. I got the impression that Minny expected me to know, that Minny thought she was co-operating with *me*."

CHAPTER FOUR

PERDITA WALKED BRISKLY along the Embankment and into the studio attached to Poldy the photographer. He had another and smarter place just off Piccadilly, but his real work was down here in Chelsea.

She met Fanny, also arriving, with a large hat-box and a small pekingese with a red bow.

"Fanny, the peke's new."

"Isn't it?" said Fanny complacently. "A present, of course, from the Baron." She was a tall, thin, elegantly dark girl.

"Oh, Fanny, should you?"

"As I don't intend to gratify his obvious desires, I should not, but as I wanted the peke, and after all, what's a dog to a man with all those dollars, it seemed a good idea to say yes. I don't think a dog commits you, not like a mink coat or a lovely little diamond bracelet."

By this time they were inside Poldy's charming Dior grey and white reception room.

Fanny at once rushed to the mirror.

"My God, I knew it, my left eye is crooked." Fanny, who was very beautiful, was always discovering different and imaginary faults in her appearance that would ruin her career.

"Darling, you look lovely, you always do," said Perdita, taking off her hat and examining her own face.

"And they could always touch it up on the prints. You know about the camera—it *always* lies."

"You look a bit peaky yourself," said Fanny, as she touched up her eyelashes with the latest dark blue mascara.

"I knew you hadn't read the newspapers," said Perdita.

"No, of course not, by the time I've got up, tidied my flat, dressed myself and done my face, and given this precious darling puppy some breakfast I haven't a minute to spare. You little debs with your lovely leisurely homes don't realise what it is to be a career girl."

"It's my lovely leisurely home that's brought the pallor to my cheeks. Look," and Perdita handed over a bundle of newspapers.

"Oh, darling, what is it, has your father been made a judge, or your mother got a divorce or has the house burnt down? Oh," she said, "*Jack* dead! I can't believe it. He wasn't that sort."

"No one's not that sort," said Perdita sadly.

"Yes, but Jack! Although mind you there's a lot must have felt like doing it."

"What do you mean?"

"Well, he was a terrific tough really wasn't he?" Fanny was turning over the papers. Even in her present state of agitation she was keeping a professional eye open, "I see there's one of me in today, wearing that nylon fur coat, not one of my best, I'm a *real* fur girl."

"Better not tell the Baron that."

"And another one of that ghastly Flowers woman. She's really looking her age now, isn't she?" asked Fanny with satisfaction. "Of course I do admit she's got absolutely no hips but what's the good of that if she's got no . . . Oh, hello, Poldy, darling. I'm glad to see you looking better today."

"Make-up," said Poldy gloomily. "Actually I'm far from well."

Poldy had left his native land at the age of six so he hardly remembered it at all, and so well had he assimilated the ways of Campden Hill and district that no one would have known him for a foreigner if he had not constantly reminded them.

"You shouldn't use make-up," said Fanny severely.

"Why not? You do."

"Yes, but——"

"For exactly the same reasons."

He glanced at Perdita. "See you're in trouble."

Perdita nodded. "Awful, isn't it. Of course I don't know anything about it. Only it's among friends. I can't really believe in it."

"Oh, what a state of happy innocence," said Poldy with a groan. "Not to believe in trouble. Well, down to business, have you got the diary with today's engagements, Perdita? And if I have to photograph Lady Pim's teeth again I shall be sick."

"Well, she is down," said Perdita. "Eleven o'clock, and you've made a note—in colour."

"Oh, how depressing," said Poldy. "That means there will be lots of pink tonsils, too. Always I say to her, a grave face today, my lady, not smiles, that lovely seriousness, and always she opens her mouth in one of those wide transatlantic smiles. She'd really be quite a pretty girl if she wasn't American."

"Lot of money," said Fanny tersely.

"And as for you, my Fanny, I shall want you in the dress from Cavanagh in two seconds. Stop gossiping and change. Perdita, hook her up, you know she isn't fit to be left with an expensive dress."

"To tell you the truth, no," said a muffled voice as Fanny struggled through the stiff creamy silk. "Pearls with this I think, don't you? Wish they were real!" and she roped the string of pearls round her pink neck.

Poldy's dressing-room was somewhat more austere than his reception-room although Perdita had made an attempt to brighten it up with a pot of flowers and Fanny herself had contributed a rug for the floor because as she said 'it was her feet that suffered most'.

"Well, I'll get them maybe when I marry Berry. After all bankers must know how to make money."

Perdita straightened the full skirt of the dress before she answered.

"I wonder if we're right, Fanny, to absolutely pursue these young men?"

"Goodness me, yes," said Fanny, wide-eyed. "If we don't someone else will. I've absolutely set my heart on Berry."

"Mm, me, too, on Tom. But I do wonder sometimes."

"My dear girl, it's perfectly fair. We shall be splendid wives. I shall be the making of Berry."

"He seems so happy as he is though. And so does Tom. It seems like robbing a baby. I've hardly got the heart." She sighed. "You haven't got the record in marriages that my family has!"

"Why worry over that? There's your gran, one of the best looking sixties in London and there's my gran still going out charing. Who did best?"

"I wish I could be as confident as you. But it's really rather shattering having one of your best friends murdered and your own mother . . ."

"Well, what about your mother," said Fanny sharply. She was clipping on great pearl ear-rings as she spoke.

"I don't know quite. But we had the police calling early this morning, and it was *her* they talked to, well he really, only one came, a young one. And last night I heard her go out of the house when I was up with Minny and the twins. I didn't hear her come back."

"I should keep that to yourself," said Fanny with the caution of one whose forebears had never called the law brother. "And I'll forget you told me. But anyway I don't suppose it's anything to do with your mother. A lovely person like her. Lots of other people knew Jack."

"So they did," said Perdita, unconsciously giving Fanny a long stare.

Fanny flushed. "I've long since got over that. You know I have. Oh, but Perdita, suppose Berry didn't believe it. Suppose he thought . . ."

"I've wondered sometimes exactly what Berry knew about you and Jack," said Perdita. "Since we *are* discussing it. Sometimes I've wondered if he did really know about you. You were very quiet you know."

"Quiet," said Fanny with a little sob. "And I used to think I must be wearing a big label with it written on me. Poor old Jack, I suppose in a way I was just as hellish to him as he was to me."

"But if Berry suddenly found out," said Perdita carefully.

Fanny was quiet. She took up the silver stole that

went with the dress. "I don't believe it. I don't believe it. You do have wicked thoughts, Perdita!"

"We've got to be prepared, Fanny. It's not only Berry, it's Tom too. Can't you see that they are the obvious people for the police to suspect? And if they can find a motive, well, there you are."

"I suppose I'd better have a quarrel with Berry or something. Oh, it'll kill me to do it."

"It might kill him if you don't. But you don't have to make a great scene out of it, of course, the police will suspect that too, just quietly freeze him out."

Fanny moaned gently. "Oh, poor Berry, he will hate it too. He's such a nervy darling. Look how he stutters. It's all his dreadful mother, spoiling him on one hand and kicking him with the other. Do you know she said to him once, 'Oh, Berry, with your eczema no girl will look at you, let alone marry you. But mother loves you.' I ask you, what a thing to say to a kid, he was only thirteen. No wonder he hates her but can't get her out of his hair. He's a nervous wreck, poor love, he *needs* me, Perdita."

Perdita looked troubled.

"Girls, girls," called Poldy from the door. "Are you ever coming out?" He was prancing round adjusting the lighting. "Now that's it, Fanny, look lively. Pose yourself against the wall with the vines on it."

"Looks more like virginia creeper," said Fanny.

"Oh, you cockney." But he smiled at her. Impossible not to smile at Fanny as she leaned decoratively against the blue panelling, let the vines fall lightly through her hands, and the pearls drip gently downwards to her waist. Perdita in her trim London dress looked at her with envy and admiration. A dress like that would certainly be a sensation in her circle. "Keep your head up."

"Do you want to break my neck?"

"Don't talk about broken necks," shuddered Poldy, "*now*."

"I didn't know Jack was a particular friend of yours."

"Oh, he wasn't. I only knew him professionally."

"Professionally!" exclaimed Perdita. "He was a gynaecologist."

"Oh, well, not like that," said Poldy annoyed. "No need to giggle, Fanny, spoils your face and gives you wrinkles besides being vulgar. I knew him in an unofficial sort of way. He used to prescribe my little tranquillisers for me, some doctors are so mean with them. Oh, I paid of course, nothing illegal or against the National Health, I'm a socialist after all, but I could have them when I wanted them. Such a relief when you consider what last season was like, the Brucker-Wykham wedding, and the Tagliatelli Masked Ball (and never shall I forget the water, drenching everything, if you are going to have fake lagoons and fountains you ought to be able to control them). So sometimes he gave me the tranquillisers and sometimes a very good little pep-up pill. I must say I shall miss him."

"Jack do much of that sort of thing?" asked Perdita, idly swinging her foot.

"Oh, I don't know. Toothy Bernard put me on to him, *he* was in rather a state himself poor thing owing to his divorce." He looked up. "Fanny, what is that dog of yours doing?"

"Well only, well only, well . . . only . . ."

"Exactly. Stop him."

"It's the vine," said Fanny. "The poor darling thinks it's a tree."

"Several trees," said Poldy. "All right leave him here. I don't want to upset you two more than I need today. Don't upset yourself too much over Jack. What you've got to grasp is that as well as being the Jack you knew and your friend, he had a life of his own that you don't know anything about. No one ever sees the whole of a person. You didn't see the whole of Jack, but something came out of his life, the part you don't know, and killed him."

"Something," shivered Fanny. "Not science fiction is it?"

"I'd like to know more about Jack though," mused Perdita. "Can't believe he really did have deep secrets and 'another life'. He was always so gay."

"Oh, my poor soul," said Poldy. "You're one of those who mistake gaiety for superficiality, and it isn't, by God, it isn't."

"Oh, don't be so Continental, Poldy. You know you're as English as we are really."

"I wonder where we could find out about Jack."

Poldy laughed. "Easy, go to that centre of gossip and information, the English pub." He looked defiantly at Fanny.

"But there are so many. I couldn't comb London."

"You infant in arms. Jack went to his local, the pub between his hospital and Pontifex Passage—the Glorious Victory."

The Victory was a dark, dusty little public house, the largest bar of which was down several steps and thus in a sort of semi-basement. Oddly enough this only added to its popularity, everyone said the beer was much better there than in the large modern hostelry round the corner. "Can't beat these old places," it was said, although in fact the two public houses were owned by the same brewers and managed by the same man and the beer was no more and no less watered down with dregs and oddments 'to keep the stocks up'. Strangers sometimes thought the Victory was named after the last war, the more knowledgeable would talk about Trafalgar, the landlord himself always looked shocked at the thought of his ancient pub deriving its name from such modern victories and let it be known that the victory in question was the Armada if not Agincourt. In fact, however, the Victory had been built in 1880 and the victory was simply that of a local prizefighter.

The two girls and the pekingese pushed through the aged and stiff swing doors into the semi-gloom of the Victory's best bar. Even though it was only just after opening time the room seemed crowded. Looking round they could see no one they knew.

"I feel a bit shy," murmured Perdita.

"Oh, rubbish," said Fanny pushing forward with the little dog. She had the animal on a long bright red leash. In their progress through the crowd the leash wound itself round several ankles from which Fanny unwound it with her vague lovely fingers. "Come along, dear," she said with her eyes fixed ahead of her. She pulled at the leash, there was a certain amount of response but not by any means what she expected. "Naughty," she said giving quite a strong tug this time.

From behind her came a long scraping sound and then a thud and the sound of breaking glass.

"Oh, Fanny," said Perdita closing her eyes, "I'm afraid you've upset someone's beer."

"Upset someone's beer," exclaimed an angry voice. "You've got me and the chair too."

Fanny spun round. "You're treading on my dog," she said fiercely.

The look of rage on the face of the unlucky man faded rapidly as Fanny made her impact. Perdita who was used to seeing what Fanny could do to people calculated that this was the fastest ever.

"Lovely little creature, isn't she?" said the man bending down to pat the dog but looking at Fanny. His gaze was filled with liking and admiration. That was the thing about Fanny, she was lovely but, you felt, utterly adorable too.

"He's a he," said Fanny with her sweet smile.

She and Perdita sat down at a little table and Fanny took off her gloves and looked around her. "Now where shall we start? All we need to do is to make a few contacts."

"You've already made one."

"Yes, he was nice wasn't he? Sometimes I regret that my heart is dedicated to Berry. But business before pleasure."

"I wonder if we've been silly to come. It seemed so sensible the way Poldy put it. He can be *so* persuasive you know."

"Not usually without a reason. That one usually has his own axe to grind," said Fanny thoughtfully. "I always think his charm is so synthetic don't you?"

The observers were also the observed. Fanny who was so used to attracting attention took little notice of it but Perdita felt uneasy. She put on her gloves and took them off again.

In the corner of the room a large man in bright coloured tweeds watched them, then picked up his drink and sat down at their table. By this time they were both drinking fruit juice, Perdita because she was nervous and Fanny because she had to think of her weight and was always counting calories. The little dog was sitting on her lap.

"I'm so sorry," said Perdita politely to the man, "but that's my foot you're treading on."

"Sorry, I'm sure. I hope it hasn't bruised it. An accident of course."

"Oh, I didn't think you'd done it on purpose," Perdita assured him. "I just thought you might not have noticed."

"Now that's my foot," complained Fanny.

"Well, that must have been wishful thinking on my part," said the man pushing his glass nearer to Fanny. "Not that I'd want to bruise a pretty little fairy like you."

"I don't bruise easy," said Fanny.

"I bet you don't. Now what about getting rid of little schoolroom here and coming out to see a bit of London with me?"

"I've seen that bit," said Fanny. "It didn't interest me."

"Here I am, just off my ship, with a nice little pile saved up (perhaps I shouldn't tell you that, but you seem a nice honest girl). We could really see places. Oh, London's a fine place to be in when you've the money. But it's not the place to starve in. I know." He moved forward to look into Fanny's face but she slid the peke forward so that instead he was staring into two bulging eyes. Disengaging himself from the fur, he went on. "Now why not come? You want looking after you know, there's some funny chaps in these parts. You'd be safe with a nice straightforward fellow like me."

"Straightforward," said Fanny. "You're so straightforward you knock yourself over coming forward. No one minds you running, my dear fellow, but there's no need to be jet propelled." And she turned to speak to Perdita. Perdita was cross.

"He meant me, do you realise, *me* when he said little schoolroom! Let's move right away."

"Oh, no, he's quite harmless," said Fanny contemptuously, casting a look at her admirer who was leaning back in his chair muttering to himself that this was the girl for him. "Hardly sober even now, you see."

It was now ten to twelve. Perdita could see the hands of the big clock in the bar. A stout, pleasant-faced girl was arranging glasses. Inspired, Perdita went up to her. "Could my friend's dog have a little water?"

"Oh, rather, love, I'll get you some? Sure he wouldn't want anything stronger? No, well I'm a real dog lover myself. Little beauty isn't it? Although mind you I like a big dog myself, a boxer say or a bull mastiff.... More protection, too, you need it sometimes going home late at night like I do."

"I live round here," volunteered Perdita hopefully. "Pontifex Passage."

"Really, dear? Well, you have had a bit of excitement round there haven't you? Of course, I knew the poor chap, we all did, in here often."

Fanny came up trailing the dog which accepted the water gratefully.

"It's a nice neighbourhood here, I'm not saying it's not, but we border on rough parts when all's said and done. And then the hospital attracts all kinds. Get lots of doctors in here we do, say they're doctors anyway, although you've got to wonder sometimes. *He* was a doctor wasn't he? A proper one, ever so kind, many a time I've heard him giving help and advice or a prescription to some poor soul. I never needed it myself, keeping healthy as I do but I could see he was doing good work. 'Quite a consulting-room this is for you,' I said to him one day, 'And so it is, Florry,' he says, 'So it is.' No money passed though, not that I ever did see. He did it all out of loving kindness."

"And that doesn't sound like Jack," muttered Fanny. "Not in the days I knew him."

The pekingese having finished the bowl of water was wandering round. He was followed by the sailor, who was carrying his drink. Across the room the man the peke had entangled picked up a little red stool and started to carry it and a glass across the room. Fanny was as usual carrying her hat-box, without which she was never seen.

The barmaid leaned across to Perdita still talking. "Jack was a nice boy you know. I didn't myself care for all his friends, but Jack himself was all right. I don't know if you could say that for Mr. Berry, and then the little foreigner, Poldy, he's a funny little chap isn't he? I always felt that the two Jack lived with weren't really his *best* friends, mind you, I'm not saying anything, but it all adds up doesn't it if a chap's murdered? And then there's the old 'un."

54

While she was speaking the pekingese had been winding its way underneath the table, it seemed very much bored by its morning and was looking for excitement. It was some time before Fanny noticed he had gone, she was exchanging eager comments with the barmaid. "Mind you, I don't want to speak ill of the dead, and I liked him but if you get yourself murdered well there must be a reason for it mustn't there? And doctors do get in with a wild set sometimes, gambling and even drugs I've heard. And he spent money like water, well it had to come from somewhere hadn't it? Tapping it somewhere you know, he must have been. You hear some funny things these days don't you about even quite respectable people like M.P.s and ladies of good family. Yes, dear, as you say . . ." Her voice stopped as she looked in horror at the picture building itself up before her.

Fanny had noticed that the peke had gone off and was giving anxious tugs at the long leash. In his wanderings the peke had wound himself round the sailor's feet, and was now once again encircling his first friend who was impeded by the stool he was carrying. Fanny too was wound round in the leash but she didn't notice this until too late. Her first tug brought a look of surprise and wonder to the man with the stool, her second a look of anxiety, and her third pull was too much for him altogether. By now she was roping in the sailor too and he although surprised was pleasantly so. The first man was dragged complete with stool towards the sailor, the sailor lost his balance quite soon and collapsed in the direction of the man with the stool. Perdita rushed forward, still carrying her glass. By this time Fanny was beginning to notice the tightness round her own feet. In addition a good many bystanders were beginning to feel the current touching them.

When the motion ended Perdita had the dog, her own gloves and Fanny's hat; Fanny had the sailor's overcoat, and the stool, and the first man had a cheese crisp, Fanny's hat-box and the sailor, who of course still had his glass.

The first man deposited his burden and looked at Fanny with less affection but an even more real admiration. "I see you weren't really trying the first time," he said.

At this point the barmaid leaned forward and gripped Perdita tightly by the hand.

"That's one of them just come in, one of the men I was telling you about. I'd like to know where he was when the murder was being done."

Tom was pushing his way through the crowd.

It seemed to Perdita that he was coming not towards her but the barmaid. But then he seemed to change his direction slightly and sail smoothly towards her.

"Didn't expect to see you here," he said. "Not your sort of thing is it?" He sounded disapproving.

Perdita did not answer.

"And Fanny too."

Fanny, all her possessions under control again, smiled at him, she liked Tom almost as much as she liked Berry.

"Well, so are you," she said.

"Oh, we all come here. Berry, Jack and I often dropped in for a drink." He paused as if remembering that this was one meeting which would not take place again. "The whole of Pontifex Passage uses it, I suppose. I've seen every one of us here, except perhaps," and he smiled at Perdita, "your distinguished father, and even *he* . . . no, I must be fair, I've never actually seen him in person."

"You're talking a lot," said Perdita.

"So I am. It must be growing on me. I've just been making a statement to the police. What is the phrase the papers use? Mr. X went to Y police station where he made a statement to the police. Well they let me out. For the time being."

"And Berry," said Fanny. "Where's Berry?"

"What a selfish girl you are, Fanny." Tom took a long drink of beer. "Berry is still there."

"No, he isn't," said Perdita. "He's coming through the door."

"Hallo, Fanny darling," said Berry, his stammer worse than ever. "Get me a drink quick. There's something nerve-racking about talking to the police even if your conscience is more or less clear."

"I'm glad yours was," said Tom, "I'm not at all sure mine is."

After Berry had held Fanny's hand and had had his drink poured into him by her loving fingers he turned to them with a serious expression on his face.

"I got a definite impression," he said, "that the police had made up their mind about one thing, that Jack was murdered and Minny frightened by someone very close to them, a person they knew, and trusted, and perhaps loved. If it was one and the same person it thins it down to a very few people doesn't it?"

He looked sadly at Perdita.

"Makes it almost a *family* business."

CHAPTER FIVE

ON THE TELEPHONE Lady Passey was being extremely frank with her daughter

"Very stupid," she declared, "I'm surprised at you. Even I know that after a murder the police keep an eye on people. Of course they followed you."

"I didn't think," said Isobel.

"So what did you do?"

"There was only me. Christopher got off. We always leave separately. I made some explanation. I think I said it was my church, and that I'd come there to think, being upset after all the trouble."

"They'd believe *that*," said Lady Passey with scorn.

"Such a nice policeman, called Sergeant Coffin. He was kind. I saw him admiring my emerald bracelet. I nearly offered it to him."

"I hope you didn't."

"No."

"Do you want me to ask Percy for help?" Percy was husband number three, now adorning a high place in the government.

"Oh, no, goodness no."

"He helped me over my trouble with Customs. But then of course I wasn't stupid."

Isobel said nothing. At all costs Percy, that inveterate gossip, must be told nothing. His well-meant aid could dish her and Robert in no time.

"Well, you'll have to tell Robert. It's the only advice I can give you. After all he's a man of the world, he won't make a fuss over a passing affair. I suppose it *is* a passing affair?"

"Oh, yes, certainly," said Isobel with a sigh. "Passing like anything."

"Well, there you are."

But since Isobel was not telling her mother everything, still less would she be prepared to tell Robert.

"And send the little girls to me. Now there's the real worry, poor little mites. But they must go up to Scotland. Ardhussey is lovely in the autumn and they can go for long walks on the hills. And how is dear Perdita? Still living riotously? Exhausted with her heavenly dissipated round of parties? Oh, to be nineteen again, and a wild young thing."

"Well, you don't do too badly do you, Mother? It *was* you in the photograph of the Fancy Dress Ball at Venice wearing tights?"

"Yes," said Lady Passey complacently, "I was quite the thing there. Of course the English are never *very* chic, but I had my success. Perdita will be the same— you were different, quieter—she's so lively. But if she's getting too much into a drink and drugs clique get her out of it that's all."

"Oh, there's nothing of that sort, Mother." Really, thought Isobel, putting the receiver down and leaning against it exhausted, Mother was getting dottier every day. Almost as dotty as the Mad Hatter.

Fragrant smells were floating over the house from Karen's kitchen. No matter what the state of mind of the rest of the household Karen would go on cooking.

In fact her dishes got more and more elaborate and recherché as her nervousness (and like all Swedes she was highly neurotic) increased. Today she was cooking chicken marengo and lemon cream surprise. The surprise would be, thought Isobel, if anyone felt able to eat it. As the succulent smells grew stronger and she realised that Karen was also cooking in wine she felt apprehensive for her household bills.

She sat down at the small rosewood desk that had been her husband's present to her on the tenth anniversary of their wedding and considered her bank statement and her bills. With mixed feelings she came to the conclusion that financially at any rate she was in a strong position. It was about the only way she was, for morally, ethically, practically she was in the soup. But it did give her a weapon to face Robert with, not a very good one perhaps, when she imagined his angry rectitude but anything was better than nothing. The wages of sin had, at any rate, been worth having, she would say to him.

What she would say to the police was, of course, a different matter.

"I wonder if I could ask to make my statement to Sergeant Coffin," she thought. "He seemed an understanding sort of man."

A little restored in spirits she poured some coffee from the small pot, covered in rosebuds, into the cup which exactly matched it; the coffee was hot and strong and gave her courage. So did her reflection in the gilt oval mirror above her desk—the Stiebel day dress might be three years old but it was very becoming and she knew it.

The house was very quiet, not even the sound of Mrs.

Daft using the vacuum cleaner disturbed her. The twins and Minny had, after much fuss, gone to school from which Isobel would presently fetch them home, and Perdita, she supposed, had gone off to work at Poldy's. Perdita had done a good deal of telephoning this morning and one call anyway had been to Poldy. Another, to judge by the speed and the language used, had been to Fanny, the girl Poldy used as a model, and who was also a close friend of Perdita's, for no reason that Isobel could discover except that she had a photogenic face and an emaciatedly thin figure, the only qualities which Perdita seemed to find essential in her friends. The third and last telephone call had certainly been to a young man, and Isobel, who knew her daughter more accurately than Perdita sometimes cared for, guessed that it was Tom.

She frowned. Tom, after all, was very much under suspicion.

The police, in the shape of Sergeant Coffin, were puzzled but working hard. At the moment when Isobel was sipping her coffee and doing her accounts, Coffin had been at work for some hours in the Divisional Office near Pontifex Passage.

"I need more detail about the people." He was turning over his notes rather wearily.

"The Divisional Office ought to have told me more," he said to himself. "If they know." He himself was based upon headquarters, the old dark buildings looking down on the river, but for the purpose of each investigation he worked in with the smaller headquarters of each division. He was a pupil of Superintendent Winter, and since he had, in spite of himself, absorbed a little of his spirit, he waged an unceasing war with each Divisional Headquarters in turn, a war which had to be tactfully kept underground but which undoubtedly added to the spirit of life for both parties as, naturally, the D.O. didn't like Winter or Coffin either. Now Coffin thought he really could detect some slackness. "An old boy like this might be just what's frightening the kid Minny." He added nothing about the murder of Jack O'Finney, he could not yet fit it into any pattern. No motive, he kept thinking, no *sane* motive, anyway.

So far there had been very little gleaning of hard facts in their preliminary investigation.

Jack was dead, and all the signs were that he had died in a fight.

It was difficult to say whom he had fought and why. *Why* might always remain obscure, thought Coffin, remembering some of the cases he had worked on, but that would not prevent them discovering *who*. And the most likely candidates seemed Berry and Tom.

Already from numerous sources the police had built up a picture of the life of the three young men in their rented house. Jack O'Finney had been living in Pontifex Passage for three years. He had been there the longest of the three young men and was in fact the person who had rented the house from a diplomat now in South America. Jack was undoubtedly a brilliant doctor in the making but there was a good deal of casual violence in him. He was, it seemed, one of those people who turn easily to force as a solution. It was not out of character that he should have died violently.

Mr. Richard Berry was a young man of impeccable background (his father was a country rector and J.P.).

He had chosen his career in banking because his mother's brother was the director of one of the large banks. Berry had a bright future and would probably end up as a knight and Lord Mayor of London. Meanwhile, when not banking, he led a gay free life and was well known in smart London circles. The only query about him was that he was leading an expensive life on very little money. "And how?" thought the Sergeant to himself.

Tom Richmond seemed an easier character to read than his two friends, he was younger to begin with and had an air of candour and honesty that appealed to Coffin. A jolly way to look, he thought, especially if you aren't. I could do with a little of it myself. However he had no reason to believe that Tom was other than he seemed. He was the only son of a prosperous business man who had been prominent in political life for years now. His working day was taken up with learning how to manage an estate in the Home Counties and how to be an architect, and his leisure wholly absorbed by Miss Perdita Duveen.

But one thing marked the characters of all three young men, each had a hot, quick temper. It could not be ruled out that there had been a fight between one of them and Jack.

On the dead man's face were the scratches and bruises he would have got in a fight. Until there was a further medical report no more than this could be said but it was unlikely that this would be contradicted.

"And one other thing about Jack O'Finney stared you in the face," thought Sergeant Coffin. "A great deal of money had passed through his hands."

The sergeant had had this forcibly brought home to him as he dressed this morning.

He remembered Jack's clothes ... A silk dressing-gown, a silk shirt and very expensive hand-made shoes.

"That's the thing, Mum," he said to his mother over his kipper for breakfast. "If I work on that fact I may get somewhere before the Old Man himself." He paused over his kipper which he was eating with extreme neatness. "*He's* worse than ever. If he does marry, Heaven help his wife, I say."

"Heaven's not likely to bother itself," said his mother pouring tea. "It never did much for me with your Dad."

"It provided you with a nice son like me, didn't it, Mum? To cheer your old age and provide you with this snug little flat." The Coffins lived in a flat high above Hammersmith Broadway, enjoying every minute of the noise and dirt which floated up to them. "This Doctor O'Finney had a lot of money, too much money."

"Where did he get it?" asked Mrs. Coffin with interest. She loved hearing about her son's cases, although she never gossiped about them.

"Doctors have the opportunity the same as anyone," observed her son cynically. "More so, perhaps."

"I will say this for you, Stanley, with all your opportunities you've always been an honest boy."

"More or less," said Coffin with a grin.

"Well, you certainly ought to be, I'm sure you had every chance as a boy. Wolf Cubs, Boy Scouts, Boys Brigade, choirboy in the Baptist *and* Wesleyan Chapel."

"That's right, Mum, I didn't have time to be wicked

and build up the connections like all my little friends did. That's why I'm in the Force now."

"I'm sure you've never regretted it. You'll make quite a name for yourself, Stanley, I've seen it in my tea-leaves."

"I like it all right. I like puzzling about people and getting the answers. It's not an easy job and not a straightforward one, everything's not a clear right and wrong, you know. I've been sorry for corpses and I've been sorry for murderers, sometimes you don't know which has had it worse."

The flippant shrill look had faded from his face and for a moment he was seen for the nervous resolute man he was.

He got up and set out on his morning work which was to call on the people in Pontifex Passage once again. He had a string of questions to ask them beginning with: "And where were you between nine and eleven on Monday morning? Can you prove it? And who did *you* see about the place between these two hours?"

The sergeant's morning did not go as he had expected, his mornings never did. To this the habits of his chief contributed their part. Superintendent Winter never believed in making life easier for anyone, least of all his subordinates. He had, therefore, left a message behind him the night before to the effect that there were certain things that must be done by Sergeant Coffin before their next meeting.

"Thinks I've got wings," muttered Coffin as he read the list. "I don't believe he really knows, poor chap, how the human body works. Statements, interviews (and why the *gas* people? Poor chap wasn't gassed, was he?). Well, I shall just have to do the best I can,

and the Old Man will have to take it philosophically."
He smiled; in other words he would do what he thought
and leave the rest. "Hi, Farrar," he called to the
constable typing in the corner, "seen the boss around?
Well, come on, have you or haven't you? Codling is
the friend not Short. In other words keep in with me,
boy, the future's with me."

"He's been in and gone off again to see the Pathological Department over the Swedenborg case."

On the sergeant's desk lay the report on the handkerchief. It was blood group O, it was therefore, in all probability stained with Jack O'Finney's blood. Minny's blood, her mother had reported, was AB. There was nothing else on the handkerchief. It had been rinsed, and badly rinsed, in water but no attempt to wash it had been found.

"Right," the sergeant nodded. "I'll just go and have a good poke round at No. 5 Pontifex Passage." He hummed. "I've had my mind on that for some time."

The almost insatiable curiosity which the sergeant possessed about other people's lives made this sort of work very enjoyable to him. He loved nosing round in other people's possessions.

Pontifex Passage was peaceful in the sun; the milkman was delivering bottles and whistling an aria from *The Magic Flute*; the road sweeper was dabbing away at pieces in the gutter and arguing with the postman who was emptying the box, and the young constable standing outside No. 5, unobtrusively on duty, was dreaming in the sun.

He gave a quick blink and an anxious look as Coffin passed him.

"Morning, son," said Coffin blithely. "Any news your way?"

"No, Sergeant, all quiet today."

"I suppose you'd have noticed?"

"Sergeant, certainly."

"Well, you can go back to sleep now."

Coffin let himself into the narrow little house. At one time it had been carefully painted in pale grey and white but three years of Jack, Berry and Tom, together with Mrs. Daft had reduced it to a sort of dun colour. There was the chip in the mahogany banister where a tough rugger player, drunk at a party of Jack's, had rushed at the stairs with a carving knife, and there was the burn on the white paint where Berry had left a cigarette when he was making a telephone call to Fanny, and as he and Fanny had then quarrelled on the telephone and then made it up there had been a nice little bonfire by the time Berry put the receiver down; and there was the spot where Fanny had stood, in the days when she was in love with Jack, threatening to throw herself over the banisters if he didn't love her, and *had* thrown a full bottle of black shoe dye.

Yes, one way and another the tenants had left their mark on the house.

Mrs. Daft had helped, of course. Her habit of quietly collecting all the dirt and rubbish and tipping it down the cellars was almost certainly responsible for the strange musty smell which hung about and which Fanny had vainly tried to exorcise with burning perfume. But, as she said, 'lemon verbena mixed with dead mouse is worse, not better'.

The house was quite empty. Berry and Tom, as

Coffin well knew, had appointments elsewhere that morning, with Winter to be precise, and he felt sure of having the house to himself.

Tom lived in the room off the narrow hall. It was the least desirable of all the rooms in the house and so had inevitably come his way, as he was the last arrival and the youngest. He himself made tentative attempts to keep the room in order but he was swamped by the equipment an architect seemed to need, by his books, and his pictures. The dominant thing in his room was a large El Greco, which he had copied himself, and it had force if not attraction. Sergeant Coffin looked at it and winced. It was not the sort of picture he enjoyed. Coffin sat down in an armchair and considered the room. It was not what he thought of as a comfortable room, perhaps even poor Tom would not have claimed this for it, but it was a man's room, a room gathered together with care and affection. Tom had put in his chairs, upholstered in thick green leather, he added a dark green carpet and a large desk. But the disorder which crept in from outside the room chilled the comfort and depressed the eye. A beer bottle lay across the pile of old newspapers, ten empty cups were ranged in a row by the desk, and a pile of Tom's clothes, neatly folded by Tom were crowned by an old, dying pot-plant. Tom had struggled with the chaos and had not won the battle.

Coffin got up and picked over the room; he found little to interest him and presently he left the room and went up to the next floor which, although reasonably clean, was disorderly with towels and soap and discarded shirts and socks lying about. Berry's room itself was precise, tidy and neat; Berry had succeeded in impressing himself upon his room. His shirts hung in rows, his shoes were arranged according to colour, and even his letters were neatly stacked. Poor Berry's nature drove him to an excessive tidiness. "Not natural," said Coffin looking at it. But even here there was a crazy note. Under the bed was a heap of dust and dirt, and the bed although tidy on top had obviously never been made.

Coffin poked over the letters thoughtfully. One from his mother, and one from his girl friend. Nothing exciting.

Jack's room had, of course, been gone over thoroughly before, it had been photographed and examined for finger-prints. There were no finger-prints other than those of the inhabitants of the house. This was probably significant, thought Coffin, although experience was teaching him that the things that looked significant rarely were so.

Still, superficially, either no one had been in the room but Jack and his friends, or the visitor had worn gloves.

The room was still marked by the struggle which had taken place in it. A chair overturned, water from a bowl of soapy water spilt on the floor, and a pile of books overset. All this, however, was only on the top of a superb almost calculated disorder in which dirty shoes stamped their outline on clean shirts, a bottle of ink dripped across a half-typed page, and a little mound of dust and dirt was neatly deposited just where anyone stepping out of bed would rest bare feet in it.

"If he'd worked at it he couldn't have done better," said the sergeant, looking at it with exasperation.

"And a doctor too." There was something terribly wrong in this house, terribly wrong.

Far away downstairs he heard, or thought he heard, a faint noise. He listened, then sped quietly down the little staircase.

The back door on to the little yard was swinging open. There was no one there. Only a large tabby cat which looked at him in a hostile fashion.

"Might have been you," he said. "Or it might not have been."

A large head, wearing a battered felt hat, popped itself over the wall. On seeing the sergeant a look of disappointment crossed the face. The sergeant went rapidly through the list of the inhabitants of Pontifex Passage and supposed he had before him Mr. Booth.

"Oh, it's not Mrs. Daft," said the head. "A pity. I'm getting hungry."

"Are you now? I'm sorry." The sergeant didn't see what the hunger and Mrs. Daft had to do with each other. He had seen Mrs. Daft very fleetingly yesterday but she hadn't looked like a cook to him. His examination of the house had convinced him that she was not much of a cleaner either.

"Oh, not your fault, me dear boy," and a large brown gloved hand—or was it wearing a spat?—straightened the hat.

"I suppose you couldn't let me come in and just have a quick dekko round your house?" asked Coffin, feeling that the moment was propitious.

"Oh, I'd be delighted. I've got some lovely things you know. Inherited of course."

"Have you now," said the sergeant surprised.

"Good," he thought, "perhaps the old boy really has got something." And he advanced in the happy anticipation of seeing something good.

Mr. Booth had given him no information at all but he had started a lot of speculation.

Coffin was in the kitchen when the bell rang.

Tom and Perdita stood upon the doorstep of Mr. Booth's house. They had rung the bell twice but so far no one had answered.

"Try again," said Perdita, and from the note in her voice it was plain that she was the one who had decided on the call.

Tom rang the bell, but still no one answered.

"I suppose he thinks there's still a parlour-maid to go and answer it," said Tom. "How mad can he get?"

"I think he's safe enough on people," said Perdita, "it's only *things* he's rocky on. Anyway, it's worth coming to see what we can find out from him. You don't want the police to suspect you, do you?"

"Not more than they do at the moment certainly." Tom was more of a realist than his love Perdita.

"You don't even want to think such things. It wouldn't look nice would it: Peer's Son in Murder Trial."

"I'm not a peer's son."

"But you know you will be after the Honours List by the time the trial comes on, if there ever is one, of course."

"Oh, there will be," said Tom grimly. "Old Man Winter won't go home without someone in his bag. Me or Berry probably."

He rang the bell again. This time there was a shuffling noise down the stairs and up the hall.

"He's coming," said Perdita. "Oh, good morning, Mr. Booth."

She was a favourite of his and although he sometimes forgot who she was he never forgot her face.

"You know you get more and more like my mother each time I see you," he said with a gentle welcoming smile. He was a small white-haired old gentleman, attired with absent-minded neatness. That is to say every separate garment was immaculately in order but it was sometimes rather eccentrically placed. Today he was wearing a well pressed grey suit and spats, but the spats were around each wrist. "Oh, you have a bonny look on you, just as Mother had. Take a look at that portrait of her," he waved his hand towards the wall by the staircase. "She would be about your age when it was done. An excellent likeness."

"Yes," said Perdita not knowing what else to say. There was no picture there. As long as Perdita had ever known the house there had been no picture there. It must have been one of the very first things to go, but there did remain an oval shade on the dark green wallpaper where once a picture had been.

The hall was dark. The curtains remained still hanging, looking as if they had been untouched for twenty years, and as Mrs. Daft was the woman about the household they probably had been. Perdita who had a slight dust allergy began to sneeze.

"Oh, the other young man did that," said Mr. Booth.

"What other young man?"

"Well, he did come in," said the old gentleman looking round vaguely. "I wonder where's he got to? He was coughing too, or did he say his name was Coffin? I get confused."

"Not in this case," said Tom grimly. "Coffin would be his name all right."

"It wasn't you?"

"Very much not me."

"Now that *is* a puzzling remark," said Mr. Booth with a frown, "I shall have to think that over."

Mr. Booth was the oldest inhabitant of Pontifex Passage and from his slip of a house he and his parents had at one time carried on a prosperous little business in making hats. Then the house had been filled with well-polished furniture and rugs and good china but the two old people had died together and without them Mr. Booth seemed lost. His house had fallen into disrepair, the furniture had got broken, never been repaired and gradually disappeared, but to Mr. Booth all was as it always had been. He would talk happily about his lovely kitchen full of his mother's nice dishes even though the kitchen was empty, dusty and mouse-ridden, and his mother's nice dishes had long since been broken by Mrs. Daft. A small income and Mrs. Daft's affectionate but muddled help kept him going. Karen too kept an eye on him and certainly some of the luscious dinner now preparing in the kitchen of the Duveens' house would be handed across to him together with a snack for Tibby the big striped cat who lived impartially in all the houses in Pontifex Passage.

"He was a policeman," said Perdita loudly. She always spoke loudly to Mr. Booth as if she could drive the shadows away with a loud voice.

"Was he now?" asked Mr. Booth with mild interest. "Would it be about the black-out?" Mr. Booth still lived in the war years which had been the death of his parents.

But he was not really interested in their answer and led them upstairs fussing round them.

"Now you did wipe your feet before treading on the Axminster I hope? It's something my mother insisted on and I try to keep up," and he glanced down complacently at the bare boards.

He then ushered them into a large and only partly furnished room. It did, however, contain the bare necessities in the shape of a couple of chairs and a deal table. In one corner was a great oak press which played some part in the hatter's former trade, indeed it still had a few pieces of felt lying on it.

"Now this is the room which worries me," the old man said, picking up an aged feather mop and banging around with it vaguely. "Somehow I feel I'm not keeping Mama's drawing-room just as she did. I can't put my finger on it, but the feeling's there."

Tom had wandered to the large bay window which commanded a view of the whole of Pontifex Passage and the house at No. 5 in particular.

"Did you see anyone going into No. 5 yesterday morning?" he asked. "Anyone different from usual that is?"

"That's what the other young man said, too," declared Mr. Booth, stopping his dusting. "Now isn't that odd. Two of you. I shall have to think about that."

"Well, did you see anyone though?"

"Well, I'll tell you what I told him: not a soul, I didn't see a soul." The old man was quite disappointed. There was no doubt if he had seen anyone they would have heard all about it.

"Brings it back to me and Berry," said Tom turning round to look at Perdita.

"But you weren't there either."

"No, very true, or we say we weren't. But the police theory is that we hung around the house, one of us or both, they don't seem to mind which, for the purpose of doing in old Jack."

"But surely the people where you work can prove you didn't do it? That you were there with them. There must be so many witnesses."

"You would think so, wouldn't you? Here have Berry and I been thinking we were pretty noticeable chaps and it seems all this time not a soul has been noticing us. 'Did you see Mr. Berry or Mr. Richmond,' they asked in Berry's bank and my office? 'Oh well, perhaps, yes,' they answer, 'we might have done, he usually is there so we suppose we did see him.' 'And are you sure it was Monday you saw him?' they ask, trying to pin them down, 'Oh, well no, might have been Sunday, Monday, or Tuesday, one day's so like another.' And there we are."

"Well, you'd think they'd have noticed Berry in a bank," said Perdita indignantly.

"Well, he's not a cashier you know, he's got a little room all his own. And he's always popping in and out. Anyway the police idea isn't that we stayed out all day, only up to midday or so. The dangerous hours seem to be between nine and twelve."

"Did the police tell you all this?"

"I worked it out."

"And where were you?" asked Perdita after a bit.

Tom looked at her.

"Ah, yes, I thought you'd get round to that." He paused. "Well, I was in and out just as I said."

They could hear someone coming up the stairs. Quick, light, but determined footsteps.

"That'll be the other young man," said Mr. Booth. "I feel almost relieved to find he *is* here, you know I'd begun to think I'd imagined him."

"Oh, you'd never do that," said Perdita.

"The human mind is a very odd thing," said Mr. Booth solemnly. "There is more in heaven and earth then is dreamt of in your philosophy—*Hamlet*. However, I'm an unimaginative man myself."

"And you'd never have imagined this," said Tom half aloud as the door opened and Sergeant Coffin stood smiling on the threshold.

"Come in, come in," said Mr. Booth, "draught isn't good for Mother's pot-plants."

Sergeant Coffin pushed his hat well on to the back of his head and stood firmly on his heels. He addressed himself to Perdita and Tom.

"Can you give me the lowdown on the old boy?" he said in a puzzled sort of way. "Here he is telling me not to trip over the umbrella stand and don't bump me head on the chandelier and there isn't a thing there. Has he been this way long or did it hit him sudden?"

"Years and years," said Perdita in her pretty voice. She remembered she liked this man. "A bomb killed his parents and then he started to forget things and live in a sort of dream world. To him it's just as it was when his mother was alive, he doesn't see how it has all changed. But he's not deaf you know, so be careful or he will hear you."

Mr. Booth turned round from fussing over the geraniums that were not there. "I can hear you now," he said with dignity. "You're like the rest of them talking behind my back, the woman Daft is always doing it."

"Oh, you like Mrs. Daft," protested Perdita. "She's a nice old thing."

"She's a servant," said the old man coldly. "I keep her in her place but it's difficult."

Sergeant Coffin looked at him thoughtfully. The old man was quite mad, madder perhaps than the young couple realised.

"You're a rum old bird you are," he said half exasperated and half amused as he watched Mr. Booth prancing round his imaginary geraniums. "What am I to make of you, eh?"

Once again the people in the big empty room heard feet on the stairs, accompanied this time by the clink of china and a muttering voice.

Mrs. Daft, wearing her usual stiff off-white overall shuffled into the room bearing a heavy tray filled with dishes of food.

Mr. Booth rushed forward joyfully. "Tomato soup, buttered sole, *sauté* potatoes, and green peas," he said uncovering dishes. "Lemon pie, cream, and cheddar cheese. Oh, goody."

"Sharp enough there, anyway," murmured Coffin. "No mistakes on that list."

"So he is sharp," said Mrs. Daft indignantly. "There's many gets the name of being not all there that doesn't deserve it. We've suffered a good deal of that in my family on account of the name. You all right my ducks?" she said to Mr. Booth. She turned to Coffin. "What he chooses to remember or not remember is his own affair. Isn't a man's memory his own?"

"Depends upon what he remembers, dear," observed Coffin mildly. "And in the case of murder it is his duty to tell the police."

"*You've* changed since you were at school," said Mrs. Daft looking at him closely. "Think I don't remember you?"

"You Eddie Daft's mother?" said the sergeant, diverted.

"I didn't know you had a son," said Perdita.

"Haven't now," said Mrs. Daft shortly.

"Yes, it was a pity about him," said Coffin awkwardly.

"Oh, I knew he'd never come back. As soon as he told me that he'd gone for a sailor I said to him you'll never come back, Eddie, and he never has. Not so far, anyway," she added grimly.

"Well, you've still got your daughter," said Coffin consolingly. "Pretty little girl, married I heard."

But they were interrupted by Mr. Booth's eagerness to get at his lunch. He took the tray from Mrs. Daft and began to arrange the dishes.

"I only use white china now," he said. "But over there I keep all my mother's best Worcester," he nodded towards a cupboard. "Show you if you like." He tripped over and flung open a door. "Lovely, isn't it," he said beaming at them.

There was no china in the cupboard but neatly arranged on the shelves were a complete set of clothes for a little girl. A round school hat, a thick cherry-red coat and little shoes.

"Those are Minny's," cried Perdita.

"Yes?" said Sergeant Coffin. "Then where's Minny?"

CHAPTER SIX

ISOBEL WAS LUNCHING with her husband. In spite of what was one way and another considerable anguish of mind she was wearing a marmalade and black wool tweed suit and looked very chic. They were eating at Homer's Nod that small but smart eating place much favoured by journalists and young career-minded M.P.s. The choice had of course been Isobel's, for Robert, left to himself would have taken her somewhere sombre but grand. Isobel saw that, true to form, Christopher was lunching across the room. He was officially back from his trip now so he could appear in public. He was lunching with Poppet Paine which angered her although Poppet was not particularly lovely or very smart. He bowed slightly. Safe after all to acknowledge that they knew each other. She caught an answering glint in the head waiter's eyes. He had caught on awfully quickly.

"Oh, were you saying something, Robert?"

"I said what arrangements had you made about the children? You not being there to keep an eye on them and collect them from school."

"Oh, I've arranged. There's Perdita you know, and Mrs. Daft."

Robert frowned. "Hope they're reliable."

"Oh, certainly they are."

"You dismiss it very easily."

"On the contrary I've given it every thought. And you *did* ask me to lunch with you."

"Yes, I wanted to talk with you."

Across the room Isobel saw this time her mother who gave her the gay little wave which meant she was coming right across to speak.

"And how is everything? You look harassed Isobel, and no wonder. I suppose you are. It's all very worrying for you, the poor little girls, although no one could call you a maternal woman . . ."

"Four girls," said Isobel.

"Yes, I can tell you are upset. There's a tiny little crease in your jacket." She looked at the marmalade and black suit and said, "I always try to have a *very* good suit. It pays in the end." And immediately the marmalade suit felt bulky and ill-fitting.

"As a matter of fact I'm having one made at Balmain," said Isobel stung into answer.

"Are you?" Lady Passey was taken aback. "However did you get all the currency?"

"Yes, how did you?" asked Robert.

"You know very well I've had that little investment in Paris-Metro Motors since Aunt Claire Felice left it to me."

"Yes, but, well, you know . . ."

"They didn't do so well when Claire had them," declared Lady Passey with envy and decision.

Isobel kept quiet.

"Well, if you've got all that money," went on her mother, "then you might afford a better wardrobe for Perdita. I've seen her in that white tulle dress from the Queen Charlotte's Ball to the Pincking hop, and you can't expect the poor girl to be a social success with grubby clothes. Not engaged yet is she?"

"Not yet, give her time."

"I was engaged in the second week of my first season," said her mother.

Yes, and look what happened, four husbands, said Isobel's expression, but she did not quite dare to say this aloud.

Her mother could read her thoughts with accuracy, however. "No, Isobel, not *really* four dear. Don't you remember, two of them were brothers, and I always think that reduces it to say—three and a half." She paused thoughtfully. "But you remember I had those very good Chinese cabinets from them."

"Yes, they are good," agreed Isobel. If there was one thing which she and her mother had in common it was regard for the value of property.

Robert looked at the two women. Seen in profile they were very alike. His mother-in-law was still a very lovely woman, with her fine long bones and pale hair, and considering how spoilt she was, remarkably interesting and intelligent. Isobel was intelligent, too, of course, he thought ruefully. "I wonder sometimes why she married me," he had said to a friend who had also known Isobel at the time of her first uneasy marriage. "Awfully difficult to think of her as married to someone else though," the friend had answered. "It's getting difficult to think of her as married at all," Robert had sighed. He echoed this sigh now. He was almost certain that she loved her family better than her possessions, more say than her *famille verte* bowl or her rosewood sofa but he felt sure that she would have viewed a fracture of the bowl with more agitation than a fracture to her arm.

"However," said Isobel's mother going back to the point from which she had started, "how is Minny?"

Isobel frowned and drew little patterns on the table-cloth with a fork. "Well. In herself that is."

"Good heavens, yes. I wasn't suggesting that there was anything wrong with Minny."

Isobel went on drawing her patterns.

"You didn't mean *that*?"

"No, I've always thought Minny a well balanced child. Still, it's all so odd you know," admitted Isobel.

"The police said the whole case, Minny being frightened, etc., is absolutely unusual," said Robert frowning. "I think they were hinting at something."

"Oh, you're so subtle," said Isobel angrily. "I think he simply meant that it was the sort of case he hadn't come across before."

"Perhaps we ought to take Minny to a child psychologist," said Robert.

A waiter hurried across the room with a message.

"Oh, it's for me I expect," said Lady Passey, "I'm pursued everywhere."

"No, for me," said Isobel, "I'm to go to the telephone."

It was possible at the Homer to see the telephone booth, a little glass cage, from the table where they sat. Robert and his mother-in-law watched Isobel take the message. They saw her sway and turn towards them.

"Something's gone wrong," said Robert getting up.

"It's Minny," cried Isobel gripping the table with

both hands. "They can't find her. She's quite disappeared."

Robert made a stiffled sound.

"No, don't say it, Robert, I know what you're thinking. But I did make what seemed good arrangements. But I shall never forgive myself now."

"Heaven help me, I wasn't going to blame you."

"This is just like you two," said Lady Passey getting up. "Selfishly baring your souls. Leave it, Isobel. The thing to do is to find Minny."

Superintendent Winter had been galvanised into fresh activity by the news about Minny. He had been preoccupied with the murder of Jack O'Finney and inclined to put aside the puzzle of Minny Duveen. Now she was right in the foreground again.

The news had been brought to him by Perdita and Tom.

"Wait a minute, let me get this straight. Don't both talk at once."

Perdita and Tom were both silent.

"Oh, come on," said Winter. "The little girl's gone, eh? You went to see her and you couldn't find her?"

"We didn't go to see her, we went to *look* for her," said Perdita. "And she's nowhere—not at school, not in the street, not in the house."

She poured the whole story out, talking rapidly and nervously. She didn't like this tall, thin, bleak man who seemed somehow to have so much of their lives in his hands. Coffin standing by confirmed it all.

"And what have you done with the old man?" asked Winter sharply.

"Got a constable sitting with him."

"Right. Well, we'll go and see him first." He turned to Perdita and Tom. "I think, if you don't mind, miss, you'd better stay with us for a bit."

"What is there about this kid Minny?" he said to Coffin as they walked through the streets.

Mr. Booth and the constable, young Evelyn, were sitting side by side at a table. They were playing patience. As they came in Mr. Booth leaned forward, put out a gloved hand and slapped the constable.

"Naughty," he said. "Cheating."

The constable looked up, caught the superintendent's eye and blushed.

"Only keeping him amused, sir. As suggested."

Winter nodded. "Now, Mr. Booth," he said. "I'm sure you understand why I'm raising the subject, but would you mind telling me why you happen to have the little Duveen girl's clothes in your cupboard?"

"It's really a very extraordinary question, isn't it?" asked Mr. Booth cocking his head on one side. "You can't know me very well if you think I'd *happen* to have clothes in my china cupboards. I'd never dream of it. Might harm the china."

"They are there, though."

"You say so," observed Mr. Booth. "Haven't seen them myself."

"But you know the little girl?" persevered Winter.

"Oh, naturally. Darling little creature. She's got the look of my little sister, just the same look in her eyes. See in that picture up there."

Winter's eyes travelled up. There was no picture.

"We didn't keep her," said Mr. Booth sadly. "She didn't last long."

Coffin moved uneasily.

"Is he always like this?" asked Winter in a low voice. The constable nodded.

"We'd better get him looked at," said Winter. "He may be dangerous. I didn't like the way he spoke about the child."

"Oh, no," said the constable quickly. "He's harmless. I swear to that."

"I tell you it made my blood run cold," said Winter later, "when he talked about his sister. I don't like this business. We must find that child."

The very advanced and experimental school where the three Duveen girls went was run by a training college for teachers. The college buildings formed part of a quadrangle and the school, with the little nursery block attended by Minny, the other side of the square.

Students went to and fro in the autumn sun, carrying books and papers, looking important and happy.

At the door of the school the policeman met Robert and Isobel and Lady Passey. They were talking to a tall, fair, flustered woman in an apple-green smock. Behind her was another woman in tears.

"I can't think how it happened, Mrs. Duveen, indeed it wouldn't have happened if I hadn't had this emergency trip to the dentist, the poor child had knocked his teeth, and of course I thought Miss Peterson . . ."

"But she didn't know and it did happen," Isobel turned away wearily.

"I can't help thinking," said Lady Passey, "that even had there been no special cause for alarm, no particular need to protect a child, there has been carelessness. To let a child of five . . ." She gave Miss Peterson a glare.

"I assure you they're often quite sensible at five," said Miss Peterson, almost weeping. "But I ought to have known that with a mother like that——"

"Oh, Miss Peterson," said the headmistress with suppressed fury, "don't be a fool."

Isobel turned to the policeman. "Well, we know now when it was that Minny disappeared. Miss Peterson gave the opportunity."

Miss Peterson gulped. "We went for a wee walk in the park you see, to see the birds and the flowers, it being such a lovely day. And naturally, of course, I kept my eye on them all the time...."

"But you didn't count them out and you didn't count them in," said the headmistress remorselessly.

"Oh, but I watched them, and they held each other's hands."

"You know my rules, Miss Peterson," said the headmistress coldly.

"Well, there it is," said Isobel. "It was in the park that Minny went off."

Winter spoke for the first time. "Who was holding Minny Duveen's hand, Miss Peterson? You say they all held hands. Who held Minny's?"

Steadied by the request for a fact, Miss Peterson thought for a moment. "I'm not quite sure, wait a minute, yes, I seem to remember two little things together in red coats. Minny was wearing red?"

Isobel nodded.

"And so it was Betty Fraser. She was the only other one."

"Well, we'll have her in," said Winter.

Betty Fraser was indeed in red. She was wearing a

bright red skirt, a sort of kilt, and a gay red and white striped jersey. Isobel closed her eyes. She remembered that Betty's father was the local football hero, and she supposed Betty must be dressed up in his colours.

Winter was plainly not at his ease when faced with a child, particularly Betty, who gave him a very cold long look and was clearly not impressed.

Coffin took over. "I hear you went for a walk this morning with teacher," he said with his best barrow-boy smile.

"Yes," said Betty. "We went. It wasn't much fun."

"And you held Minny Duveen's hand?"

"She held mine," corrected Betty. "I'm bigger than her."

"So you are."

"How old do you think I am? I'm big for my age."

"Oh, er, I should think you were a big five."

"I'm six," said Betty coldly.

"We want you to tell us when Minny stopped holding your hand and went away."

Betty looked at him. "My father says Minny's not right," she announced.

"What?"

"My father says Minny's not *right*."

"Well, we'll leave that shall we? Just tell us when Minny went away." Coffin was hissing the words.

"My father says the police have got it all wrong."

"She's got a splendid command of English," said Winter thinly. "I congratulate you, Headmistress."

"She seems to have learnt most of it from her father."

"This isn't getting us anywhere," said Isobel.

They stood in a little group and looked at each other.

"Minny never said anything," declared Betty suddenly. "She never did talk much. But I knew she didn't mean to come back to school with the rest of us. She brought her purse with her money with her."

"So now we know," said Winter, "that at least the child went off of her own free will."

"We still don't know when and where she went," said Isobel desperately. "Betty, just where did Minny leave go of your hand? Can you remember?"

"Where?" asked Betty in surprise. "Why by the park gates, of course."

There was a moment of complete and utter silence.

"Yes," said Winter. "Well, of course, it's obvious I suppose now that the child would leave by the park gates. Silly of us really not to think of it for ourselves." It was utterly unprecedented for Winter to describe himself as silly. When he did so the extreme seriousness of the situation was apparent to Coffin, if indeed it had not been so before. "Where was she going though?"

"She had tickets from the tube in her pocket last time," said Isobel looking out through the park gates to where the tube station stood. She was already walking in that direction.

"Better leave this to us, ma'am," said Winter, and he put a hand on her arm. She threw it off and marched forward.

The rest of them, Tom, Perdita, Robert and Lady Passey, stood with Sergeant Coffin in a little huddle by the gates and watched the superintendent and Isobel go into the tube station. They were gone for some time, the minutes dragged. At last they came back.

"Got nothing," said Coffin at once, he could read Winter's expression.

"They knew nothing there, saw nothing, and got nothing to say. Like the three monkeys," reported Winter sourly. "If the child went there, but I don't believe she did, they didn't see."

Coffin spoke to Isobel, "There are other tube stations within walking distance. We'll get them all covered. I think you'd better get home, Mrs. Duveen." He nodded slightly at Robert.

When he had a chance to speak to the superintendent without anyone hearing he dropped his voice and said, "But I think we're going about this the wrong way. We've got to face it. Those were the kid's clothes in that cupboard. Why are we pretending she's wandering around without them? How did the clothes get there, and why? If we answer those we might find out more about what happened to Minny." He paused and said reluctantly, "It doesn't look, does it, as though the kid's alive."

"You covered the Booth house thoroughly?"

"There's one thing you can be sure of, Minny Duveen's not in No. 4 Pontifex Passage, alive or dead."

"Just her clothes," said Winter.

"Just her clothes."

Nothing more was said. Both policemen knew that this was bad enough.

Isobel turned back towards the two policemen. "I can't just go quietly back to the house. There's one other place to go and that's the park."

"We have men there, you know," said Coffin. "First

thing we did." He himself no longer expected to see Minny alive, and he wanted to spare Isobel.

"I'm going."

Inevitably they all came with her, Tom holding Perdita's hand, Robert still carrying his mother-in-law's fur stole which he had picked up in the first rush from the Homer Nods, and Lady Passey letting little trickles of tears run down her cheeks. Isobel was adamantine and cold.

The little park encircled by its ring of green railings, and inside them an inner circle of poplar trees, was empty; they could see from one side to the other, and no one was there except a park-keeper and a distant policeman. Betty had had her reasons when she said 'it was not much fun'. It was a dull little park and to the party which now surveyed it it was also a sinister one.

Tom was not surprised to see the sleepy park-keeper dreaming by a rubbish bin not far away. He opened his eyes at the noise of the arrival and watched them walk towards him.

"I've told the police, lady," he said to Isobel when she questioned him, "I saw all the little girls but I didn't notice one special."

"This one was wearing red," pleaded Isobel.

"I know the little girl. I've often seen her. I know about all the trouble you've been in. But I never saw her this morning. That's gospel."

Winter gave him a hard look. It was always possible, he thought, that the man might be concealing something. In this sort of case people, alas, did.

Coffin thought the keeper was speaking the truth.

"You know," he said, "I think perhaps we asked Betty Fraser the wrong question."

"What do you mean?"

"Perhaps we better go back and try Betty again."

Betty had finished her school dinner, and was resting, together with her little playmates. She was roused from her sleep, however, and came out to see them, a stocky pugnacious figure in her red clothes. Only half-awake, she was inclined to be irritable.

"Betty," said Coffin, "you told us that Minny left you by the park gates. Did she ever go into the park at all?"

"No," said Betty in a surprised tone at such stupidity, "I told you, she run off at the gate."

"You must have seen where she went?"

"She just run."

"She ran? Not walked?"

"No, she run?"

The words summoned up a picture of Minny's little figure running forward into what?

"The way I see it," said Coffin slowly, "is that Minny didn't just get bored with the walk, and no one lured her away, she never went for the walk at all. She left at the point where she was nearest her way home. She didn't run away, she ran home. She ran to Pontifex Passage."

He looked at Isobel with sympathy.

"After all, that is where we found her clothes."

"Mrs. Duveen," said Winter, but reluctantly, "I think we ought to ask you to see these clothes. Your eldest daughter identified them, but it's possible you might have more to add. Do you mind?"

"Where are they?" whispered Isobel.

"Still where they were in the cupboard at Mr. Booth's."

When Isobel saw the clothes she picked them up and turned them over and over in her hands in a puzzled sort of way.

Then she sat down and covered her face with her hands.

"Get a glass of water," said Winter quickly.

"No, no water," said Isobel. Amazingly she smiled at them. "Perdita should have known," she said. "Those *were* Minny's dress and coat, they are the cherry-red shade I liked to dress her in, but these are her old clothes. She hasn't worn these for over a year."

Coffin who was standing looking out of the big bay window heard these words almost without surprise, for just as Isobel began to speak, he looked over the hedge which divided the houses and in the garden at No. 2 he saw a small figure dressed in red. Minny was digging in her garden.

"I've been here all the time," she said puzzled when they questioned her.

"But why did you leave school, why did you run away?" The tears were falling plentifully from Isobel now.

There was a very long pause. "Man," said Minny. And she turned back to her digging.

"What sort of man?" cried Isobel. "Who? What's he like? What sort of face?"

Minny was silent. Then: "No face," she said, and went on with her digging.

CHAPTER SEVEN

"IT'S A NASTY business," said Winter. "There's something unpleasant about this trouble with the child. There's constantly the feeling of a threat to her and yet it comes to nothing every time."

He was not alone in his unease. All over London people began to talk nervously and yet with curiosity about Pontifex Passage. Mothers with young children watched over them sharply.

The iron character of Superintendent Winter (whether he modelled himself upon the first Duke of Wellington his colleagues never knew but they felt that he had much the same attitude towards them that the Iron Duke had towards his troops. Winter never actually called them a scum of men but they were sure the sentiment was there all right) stood the strain of waiting for the Passage case to be resolved. Winter never used the word 'cracked' of a case like some of his transatlantic fellow policemen. A case simply bent before his relentless pressure. He was waiting for it to bend now.

"It's getting on my nerves," admitted Coffin. "That poor little kid."

"There's a good deal more in it than we've seen yet."

It had been established that Mr. Booth must be ruled out; the doctors insisted that he was not violent and also that he could not have killed Jack O'Finney without having killed himself. "His heart wouldn't stand it," the doctor said.

"You don't mean the child's making her story up? Not that little kid?"

"Someone's deceiving us," Winter pointed out gloomily. "And I've never learnt there was an age limit."

"But five years old . . ."

"I saw a kid of six in the courts the other day. He was dealing in scrap iron. He picked over the rubbish dumps and dustbins to see what he could get and then sold it. Drove a good bargain too. Then he went a bit too far one day when his profits were dropping and sold his brother-in-law's bike. It wasn't worth much but it was worth a bit more than he got for it, but whatever he'd got it wouldn't have been enough in the circumstances, because his brother-in-law wasn't very fond of the family he'd married into, and was only too glad to make trouble for it: he went for the police and his ma-in-law went for him with a hammer—he had a thin skull and ma had a heavy hand so all in all no one was better for the scrap-iron merchant's dealings, least of all the scrap-iron dealer himself who finished up without a brother-in-law and without a mother."

"Of course I was no angel myself," said Coffin reminiscently.

"Oh, children aren't what they were in my day," said Winter.

"Oh, I don't know," said Coffin vaguely. "Look at Fagin."

Superintendent Winter's tales of his childhood were ill received by his subordinates who thought he made them up and certainly they did vary. Sometimes he spoke of himself as having struggled through searing poverty with no help except his own strength of character. He was a self-made man he used to say. (A pity he finished the job, was his friends' reaction to this saga.) Then again sometimes he spoke of himself as the product of a loving sheltered background with a thoughtful Mother and a hard-working Dad. (They didn't shelter him enough, was the comment on this version, ought to have put the lid right on him and left it there.)

"My dates are a little bit later," said Winter sharply. The bleak wind of age was blowing on him these days and he didn't like it.

"More like little Lord Fauntleroy," said Coffin, even more vaguely.

Winter tightened his lips and changed the subject. "You've looked over the statements, I suppose. Any leads? Anything strike you?"

Coffin admitted reluctantly that nothing did. "We're getting on with all the routine checking of course."

"I'm inclined to agree with you. Nothing significant has emerged yet. And that goes for the statements too. As far as possible everyone has avoided anything in the nature of a concrete fact, date, or time."

"Well, they are a dreamy lot."

"Don't you believe it. Got their heads fixed on as well as the next. Don't be put off by that vague manner. Sharp enough underneath. Look at Mrs. Duveen, all lazy and polite. She was taking everything in though. Well, so was I. And I'd like to know why she went off to Paris three times in as many months."

"Did she though?" Coffin was interested.

"The Scandinavian maid said so (no love lost there mark you) and I checked with the Customs at London Airport: they knew her at once. Striking woman. No good in Paris you know," said Winter seriously. He brooded, and Coffin could see that his stern upright English Puritan mood was coming on. "I was in Paris once."

"Yes," said Coffin briefly. "I know." Winter's trip to Paris was part of the saga too. He had gone gloomily and had returned still gloomy but close observers, and all his associates were forced to be close observers of his moods, detected a difference in the gloom, not perhaps a lightening, but at least a lifting of the shadows. Afterwards he was reported to have said the French were 'foreign', but all the same it was thought he had enjoyed himself.

"And I'll tell you something more," said Winter. "So did Jack O'Finney."

"What? With her?"

"I don't know if he was with her or not," said Winter, darkly. "That'll have to be gone into. By you. But he went once to Paris and his dates there coincide with her second visit. I checked the whole crowd while I was at the airport and he was recognised. And his passport was stamped."

"And not the only one," went on Winter pursuing his own line of thought. "They say she's been going around with Christopher Cobley, the M.P., too."

"People do go to Paris to see the sights or on business," protested Coffin. "Look, you went yourself." Privately he thought the old boy was more than a bit old fashioned. "After all, why leave London? They say there's more vice here than in any other capital city."

"I'd like to see a few more passports," muttered Winter. He shuffled the papers on his desk. "But when all's said and done the likeliest prospect is one of the two young men in the house with O'Finney. There was a fight and one of them killed him. Fits in with the facts as we have them so far you know."

"No motive," said Coffin succinctly.

"You don't need much."

"We should have to show something for the Public Prosecutor."

"Oh, well, a sudden quarrel over a girl, money, anything."

"I never like these circumstantial evidence cases," murmured Coffin. "Especially," he went on, "when we haven't got any."

Winter looked down at the statement he had just re-read. "You know I think we missed something. We ought to have talked more to the schoolmistress called Peterson. There's something wrong there." He pointed to a sentence in the statement. "Notice what she said about the mother."

The Duveen family huddled in the gay little house. In the kitchen Karen and Mrs. Daft consumed cups of tea and thick rich pastry. Karen's point of view was that this could only happen in England: "It is well known," she said, "that in England you murder and kidnap children all the time. Oh, there is something odd going on here," and she took another pastry.

"Something odd is right," grumbled Mrs. Daft,

stirring her tea. "And the police don't know everything either. Look at 'em—can't make up their minds whether one of the young men killed Dr. O'Finney or whether it was poor old Booth. Even as it is they've practically frightened the old boy into a fit. Not his fault if the police find the kid's clothes hidden in his house. In the end I said to that tall gloomy fellow called Winter, 'Go away,' I said, 'and stop pestering the poor old chap. Anyone can see he's as gentle as a bird.' 'Not all birds is gentle,' the copper says, 'Look at vultures.' Still off he went. You have to speak up to the police."

"He left a constable behind," observed Karen. "And one here too."

"Well, he needn't think it's my lady," said Mrs. Daft up in arms at once at any slur on Isobel, whom she adored. "She's a beauty she is and good too. Not many like her." Isobel had showed many kindnesses to Mrs. Daft; she gave her good wages, often let her have the children's clothes to sell, and in return received the deep admiration of Mrs. Daft who was a natural hero-worshipper.

Upstairs on the top floor Robert faced a hostile audience. He had all the children with him, including Perdita, and he was trying to ask them a few questions.

"Oh, stop walking the floor and looking like Torquemada," said Perdita. She took out the flat tortoise-shell cigarette case that her grandmother had given her for Christmas, and lit a cigarette. "And please don't say 'No smoking in the nursery'. The twins love it, don't you twins?"

Minny sat on the floor turning over the pages of a picture book and the twins licked at their paint brushes as they attempted a violent water-colour picture of their house on fire. Being twins they worked, although irritably, at the same picture. "It's a fire," they said, "and we really need more water to do it justice."

"Justice is not being attempted," said Perdita. She looked at Robert. "He's a lawyer. Don't ask too much of him." Then she looked again at her stepfather of whom she was very fond and her temper retreated. "Don't worry so much, Robert. Honestly, I'm sure it'll all come all right. I'll do anything I can to help."

"I know you will. You might make a start on this nursery."

"Of course I will." She put out her cigarette and stood up willingly enough. "Not really a job after my heart but I'll try. I must say this place has gone to seed since my time."

"You weren't a baby in this nursery," said one of the twins.

"Certainly I was. Much you know about it. Not such a tiny irritating little baby as you and your sister were, but still I was here. I can remember that rabbit," and she pointed to a picture of a rabbit.

"*My* rabbit," said Minny, her face puckering.

"Please, Perdita, take Minny down for a walk in the garden and let me talk to the twins," said an exasperated Robert.

"All right." Perdita stopped her efforts at cleaning up with relief. "You won't reduce that tough couple to tears the way you did Minny."

"I did not make Minny cry."

Robert had spent some time anxiously and almost angrily trying to make Minny talk to him; he felt sure that some information could be extracted from her, or from the twins. It was no use Minny hiding behind this blank wall and simply saying "Man". But at the end of an hour he had admitted defeat. He was an affectionate man, and he could not bear to bully or threaten the little girls, but there were moments, looking at their blank eyes, when he felt tempted to do so.

Isobel was lying down, she had collapsed into a sort of hysteria. "No face," she said in a choking voice, "but that's rubbish. Everyone has a face." After a rest and a strong drink she was quiet and restored but still not herself. Robert had left her lying in bed wearing an eau-de-nil satin bed-jacket and lying against a sun-yellow cushion in padded brocade, a gift, needless to say of the luxurious Lady Passey. She was reading Charles Morgan ("So soothingly unreal, you see") and smoking. The consumption of cigarettes in the Duveen household must have doubled overnight, Robert reckoned.

At intervals the telephone rang and it was either Lady Passey, or the police, or the Press. All three were keeping a watchful and worried eye on Pontifex Passage and on Minny Duveen in particular.

Robert himself had telephoned his chambers to say that he would not be appearing and had tried to think about Minny. He would understand more about Jack O'Finney and the murder he felt when he understood more about Minny.

Poor Minny, however, was disappointingly difficult to understand. He had never properly grasped before what an elusive child she was. He was a loving father but a busy one. He tried not, as he often said, 'to leave it all' to Isobel. In fact he prided himself on taking an active interest in his children, but the truth remained that he knew little of them. They met at breakfast and then hardly at all for the rest of the day; he certainly chose their schools and advised Isobel about their holidays by the sea, but he never talked to them. A professional talker by trade he liked to be silent when at home. But just as you got to know a witness by what you might call conversation, so apparently was this the way you got to know your children; and Robert had neglected to do so. Paradoxically enough it was Perdita whom he found he therefore knew best because he had listened to a good deal of her prattle which he often found amusing; he admired her obstinate and determined character which, like her grandmother, she hid beneath an air of charming prettiness. As to the others he recognised sadly that he loved them but hardly knew them.

On this occasion he got no change out of the twins and Minny at all.

Minny no longer even repeated the word 'man' but stared at him silently then went back to her book. Yet later on he heard her chattering away with Mrs. Daft.

"Can *you* get anything out of her, Mrs. Daft?" he asked.

"Oh, no, sir, I wouldn't think it right to try. She'll get no rest, poor little thing, with us and the police on to her all the time. We've asked her once (some of us more than that) and she's told us all she can. Leave her be."

The terrible twins were, of course, a dead end conversationally as always. No one ever quelled their resolute spirits. Robert thought that in them he caught a glimpse of himself as he used to be before his war service and his subsequent career had quenched him.

He recognised sadly that he had been quenched and was the duller for it. "I suppose I only had a certain amount of light and amusement in me and it all got used up," he told himself. The twins must have inherited their charm from Isobel because they were pretty and delightful, and also, their father suspected, clever.

He thought this more than ever at the end of his questions to them.

"But we don't know anything," they repeated. "Of course we don't. Nothing frightened us you see and we don't know what frightened Minny."

"But surely you must have seen something? What I can't understand is the way you all seem to live in a dream. I don't believe it."

The twins looked at each other. It was clear that they found Robert equally unbelievable.

"Do you remember the time our hamster, Peter, got lost?" said the elder twin after a minute.

"Yes, of course. He was lost for weeks, wasn't he?" Robert had not regretted the departure of Peter who was an aged and smelly animal, almost bald and entirely unlovable in his eyes although not, it seemed, to the children.

"He got lost just when you said he ought to be destroyed," said the elder twin severely.

"So he did," said Robert absently.

The twins looked at him exasperated; they thought him very stupid. Indeed they had relied on this trait to prolong Peter's life.

"He was never lost at all," said the twin. "He lived all the time at the bottom of the garden. But we never let on did we?"

"No, you didn't. But what has all this got to do with Minny?"

They looked at Robert in despair for such dullness and density. It seemed impossible to them that this large stupid creature could be their father when they were so intelligent. Probably they were changelings.

"We were fond of Peter," they said at last. Then they went back to their games which had now extended to painting the nursery walls about which they were counting, and accurately, on their father simply not seeing.

"Yes, thanks, I get you," said their father leaning back. "I see what you mean. Minny's affections are involved. Well, thanks for the tip. And I shall remember to keep an eye on you two in the future," ended Robert, but forgetting to do it in the present and leaving the two painting the wall ochre red in stripes.

His daughters looked at him cheerfully and went on with their painting.

How many people was Minny fond of? Robert asked himself. And knew that he could number her affections on the fingers of one hand. In this way Robert, like the policemen earlier, came to the conclusion that the answer must lie within his own family. He went downstairs to find his wife.

Isobel was still lying in bed, talking in a dreamy way to Perdita.

"I feel so relaxed and idle," she said, "as if nothing really matters any more. And I feel a silly desire to giggle. I haven't felt like giggling since I was a girl at school. Must be the doctor's drugs."

"Sounds more like brandy," said Perdita.

"Really? Did I have brandy."

"Someone must have, I think. There's a whole empty bottle by your bed."

She and her mother giggled. A crisis always brought them together: when all was well the faults they had in common kept them apart. Now they were almost happy.

"By the way, is it true you never wear anything but your white dress to parties? Granny says she keeps seeing you in it."

"Yes, she does rather haunt me, I must say," said Perdita gloomily. "Extraordinary how our age groups clash. I'm always running across her."

"But is it true about the dress?"

Perdita blushed. "It is rather a favoured dress. Perhaps I have worn it rather a lot. Tom likes me in it, he says girls my age ought to wear white. And then the black and gold dress went tatty so soon. I look *rusty* in it."

"Yes, I told you at the time it would never do."

"I admit the white is on its last legs, though," said Perdita looking at her mother hopefully. "Fanny has some gorgeous clothes and so does Gran. She might pass some on, I'm about her size."

"I'll buy you a new dress," said Isobel; she was conscious she had treated her daughter badly.

"Really? Can I have one of the heavenly new ones with no waist and all the emphasis on the back? Oh, bliss."

"Heavens, no, when will you learn to distinguish between what's fashionable and what's actually being worn?" Then she realised that she was treating Perdita in the way her mother had so often treated her. "Never mind, darling. I'll tell you what, I'll take you to my best dressmaker, the grand one, and make her show you some clothes and you can bring Tom—that is if you think he'd like it."

"Oh, he'd adore it, Mother, what a treat." Perdita did not say, although she thought it, but can you afford it, mother? She thought it, and wondered. And worried.

Then Isobel sighed. "I'd forgotten for a moment how ghastly things were. But now it's all come flooding back."

"Have some more brandy."

Isobel looked at the bottle. "You know that wasn't me. I think it must have been your father."

"Or Mrs. Daft. She's going around looking hunted. Thinks the police are after her no doubt."

"She does take things to heart, poor old thing."

"But not Robert." Perdita was surprised and half amused. "Not drinking brandy."

"He really is worried."

"When I left he was conducting a sort of inquisition in the nursery. He won't get anywhere of course. Those kids won't talk. They wouldn't say anything if they knew anything and how could they? I don't understand Minny. Do you?"

"I'm her mother," said Isobel shortly.

"You're mine too if it comes to that."

"Meaning?"

"Oh well, Mummy, let's face it, I've had a few thoughts and wishes you've known nothing about, at least I hope not. You can't read me like a book, and you can't Minny."

"She's only five."

"I know. We keep saying that. But she's old for her age." Perdita leaned forward and put her hand on the eau-de-nil silk. "It's absolutely no good pretending is it?"

"I shall get up," said Isobel. "I don't feel quite so comfortable as I did before. Get me some clothes."

Her daughter went to the wardrobe and started choosing clothes. "Here you are, this tweed dress always suits you, especially if you put on a bright lipstick. I know it's new, but might as well wear your best—keep your morale up." She was getting out shoes and a belt. "I wish you and I could have some mink. It's getting cheaper you know," she said seriously, "the price of mink is really dropping."

"Good," said Robert coming in and shutting the door with a small bang. "We're really beating inflation then. I want to talk to your mother, Perdita. I thought you were looking after Minny."

"All right," said Perdita coming away from the wardrobe. "I can take a hint, Robert, no need to make it a bloody great shovel." Any other time her adjective would have provoked an explosion. This time to her disappointment nothing happened: Robert simply had not heard. For a moment Perdita looked very like the twins.

"We really must talk," he said to Isobel, as the door closed behind the girl. "I have let you go your own way, although this past year I have wondered exactly what that path was. Still I haven't been an interfering husband, have I?"

"No, far from it. Very far indeed."

"Now we must talk plainly. I suppose I've never really done that before."

"You underrate yourself," said Isobel dryly. "You have always made yourself very plain indeed."

Robert looked baffled. This look was very often caused by his wife. She was more trouble to him than any judge. He knew their little prejudices and unreasons well enough; he was beginning to suspect that the trouble with Isobel was that she was terrifyingly reasonable.

He started again. "But now I must know, for the sake of us all, what you are hiding from me."

"Not from you specially, Robert," said his wife. "I ought to tell you that."

"Then I ought to tell you this: your mother asked me yesterday if I was considering a divorce." He added grimly, "She had a name to offer me too."

Surprisingly, Isobel grinned. "It's rubbish you know," she said. "There's nothing in it. Not in that way."

"No, I never supposed there was. I flatter myself that the girls and I mean something permanent to you. However it means something." He spoke in a level tone, trying for no emphasis, just as he might put a point to a witness he knew he was going to trap. "Don't worry," he seemed to be saying, "but if you look down now at your feet you'll see they are near a great big hole." It was this trick which made him successful where he might often have failed to produce what he wanted.

"It's Christopher Cobley of course, not poor Jack O'Finney as you once seemed to think. I hoped it would not come to telling you. We've done our best, too much so perhaps, to keep it quiet."

"Oh, Isobel, Isobel, I could have forgiven you so much more than that. How curious if you should turn out to be stupid in the end."

"Yes," said Isobel steadily, "but unluckily I'm not stupid you know. I counted on your forgiving me."

"Then . . . ?"

"I intended one relationship to cover up another. I suppose you might say we entered into a business relationship too, and that I *did* intend you should never hear about." She sighed. "I needed money you know. We both did. This house doesn't run on a song. Four girls."

"You'd better tell me."

"We've been speculating in francs. I had the foreign capital, you see, and Christopher had the information and poor old Jack had the contacts. All quite illegal and from Christopher's point of view not quite what he should have been doing with the information he'd picked up on that blasted Committee of his. So naturally his thinking he was in love with me was a splendid cover up."

"You are stupid after all," said Robert. "My God."

Then he said: "Well, I can see you wouldn't want that to come out. And now Jack is dead. Murdered. Yes, you certainly put the cat among the pigeons. And what a pigeon! Ripe for the plucking. There isn't one of us that will not lose something. One pigeon already has—Jack."

"It must be for some other reason Jack was killed." Isobel was insistent. "He was a curious person. He played along with Christopher and me but there was more in him than we ever understood. He wasn't a straightforward person. And although he spoke English I sometimes thought that it wasn't the first language he'd learnt."

Then she dropped her voice and almost whispered to Robert. "And then, all along, I've had this strange feeling about Minny. I've felt that whatever she's been up to or has had happening to her she has thought that she has been helping *me*."

The headmistress of the school where the children were pupils was a woman after Winter's own heart. She looked a neat, quiet, well-rounded woman dressed in an unexpectedly smart grey dress with gold ear-rings and her handshake was the first hint you had of her character—it gripped the hand like a set of well-padded little pincers.

Coffin took his hand away and nursed it gently, eyeing Mrs. Moss with respect. A woman like that could certainly teach the children a great deal, but he hoped she knew her own strength. Still, no doubt it was a splendid idea to let the children start out in life with a woman of metal, there would be no danger then of letting them run away with the idea that life would not come out and treat them rough on occasion.

She eyed them squarely. "Your business is my business," she seemed to be saying. I like a woman who knows her own mind, thought Coffin, provided she doesn't know mine too. He rather feared that Mrs. Moss knew all his mind and the superintendent's also.

"I'm afraid Miss Peterson will be very busy now," said Mrs. Moss. "Hardly a good time for you to see her. Later perhaps."

Winter insisted. An obstinate look was spreading over his face.

"Oh, very well," said Mrs. Moss. "You will have to

see her in the company of thirty mixed infants, you understand that?"

"Mixed?" questioned Winter, wondering if this was the term for a sort of very juvenile delinquent.

"Boys and girls," said Mrs. Moss. She did not quite say "How stupid you are," but she certainly looked it.

"Perhaps you could keep an eye on the children while I have a word with their teacher," said Winter mildly.

"You are mistaken," said Mrs. Moss, "if you think Miss Peterson is teaching them anything."

"Well, whatever she is doing," said Winter irritably.

"She is observing," said Mrs. Moss. "This is free expression day. The teacher merely stands by and watches, taking it all in, of course, in the light of her trained intelligence, and the children play or work as they please. If I may so put it, the children are teaching *her*."

Winter pursed his lips. "Well, perhaps they could teach *you* for a change, and I could have a go at Miss Peterson."

Coffin had been watching with mounting apprehension this clash of the giants. He waited now to see what Mrs. Moss would say to this sally. Surprised, he saw her beginning to smile. He wished he could say the same for his own champion: no hint of a smile there.

"Yes, Inspector," she said. "I am not above thinking the children could instruct me."

"Superintendent," said Winter before he could stop himself.

"You mustn't be proud you know," went on Mrs. Moss. "It is a fault I am prone to myself, so I know the dangers."

"Round two to Mrs. Moss," thought Coffin, who was keeping a mental score-card. Really she was scoring too fast. But she had tired of the game now, and advanced to a new victim.

"Ah, here is Miss Peterson."

Miss Peterson came down the corridor at a fast trot. Today she wore a gay sage-green smock but it was speckled with red. Looks more as if she's been observing a bull-fight than a class of little 'uns, thought Coffin as he took in her fast breathing and agitated air.

"Everything going well?" asked the headmistress kindly.

"Oh, very well," said Miss Peterson still breathing heavily. "The whole class have decided to paint with poster paints, so gratifying you know to get a spirit of working together, and little Sammy Potter has just thrown a tube of red paint at the wall which in view of his *sad* inhibitions in the past must be taken as a definite step forward."

"Oh, splendid," said the headmistress. "Try to get him to share his fun next time. Throwing a whole tube just by yourself is still a little selfish." Coffin saw with respect that she was a woman of humour who could laugh even while she esteemed. For later events showed that she did in fact esteem her devoted if sometimes exasperating assistant.

This was too much for Winter. "Madam," he said. "In my opinion the whole of civilisation depends on children acquiring as many inhibitions as possible."

"Oh, it's people like you that have caused all the dreadful troubles and wars in the past," began Miss Peterson fiercely.

"I'm afraid you yourself, Superintendent Winter," said Mrs. Moss with sympathy, "must be regarded as a seriously *thwarted* personality."

"Probably an unreconciled sexual block," said Miss Peterson earnestly. "Jealousy of the father-figure in youth no doubt. Tell me did you ever ask your mother if . . ."

Coffin stepped forward hastily; someone must protect his chief or he would have apoplexy. But, "My father died before I was born," he heard Winter say, and he received this addition to the Winter saga with interest and disbelief.

"I suggest, Miss Peterson," said the headmistress, "that you must not rule out some serious physical deficiency." She gave a quick amused look at Winter. "For Sammy Potter I mean, of course," she added demurely.

"Yes, I might pursue physical development in comparison with siblings," mused Miss Peterson. "I've had a good deal of success with that in the past."

"Sibling means brother or sister," interpreted Mrs. Moss kindly to the policemen. "Sammy Potter is an only child," she observed in an aside to Miss Peterson, thus showing she was bowling at both sides.

Don't press the old man too hard, Coffin wanted to warn them, when he heard Winter come up with his blow.

"And what success would you say you have had with Minny Duveen?"

There was a moment of complete silence. It was a silence which hinted at a good deal to an experienced policeman. Coffin knew intuitively that the case was moving forward. "My God, the old man's got on to something," he thought with a nip of excitement.

"A most interesting behaviour pattern," said Miss Peterson uncertainly.

"We mustn't be foolish, Miss Peterson," said the headmistress regretfully. "Superintendent Winter is investigating a murder, he wants information, not an analysis." She turned to Winter. "Miss Peterson thinks the child was in the grip of a behaviour pattern, and I think she was in the grip of a situation. Something she could not control.

"I have no idea what that situation was," she added. She gave a sharp look at Miss Peterson and motioned her to be quiet. This was not lost on Winter.

"I'm of your opinion," he said to her, "but you do me an injustice. I am interested in behaviour patterns. Or behaviour, anyway. If it is at all odd. Miss Peterson, why did you say: 'But what can you expect with a mother like that?'"

"I don't know. Did I say that?" said Miss Peterson with a white face. Mrs. Moss made a sound under her breath and moved closer to the woman.

"Like what, Miss Peterson? What do you know of Mrs. Duveen?"

"Only what everyone knows," said the teacher with her voice rising. "She's an idle, wicked woman."

"I don't know," said Mrs. Moss, with gentle emphasis. "Be quiet, Miss Peterson."

"Miss Peterson," said Winter, "it seems to me very extraordinary that an experienced, even enthusiastic, teacher should let one of her small class escape her on a walk. I can't believe that you didn't automatically keep an eye on *all* the children."

Miss Peterson made a choking noise of protest.

"You were glad Minny went off, weren't you? In your heart you wanted her to go."

"She was like her mother," gasped Miss Peterson. "I didn't trust her. I saw her go off. She was a naughty little thing. Both those two were nothing but a worry to the doctor. I used to see them together."

"And what do you know about the doctor?"

"Dear Dr. O'Finney, he was a wonderful doctor. He treated me at the hospital. He deserved all the love and affection he could get. But not from her. Not from her."

"You were jealous," said Winter slowly. "Of mother and daughter."

Mrs. Moss put her arm round Miss Peterson. "You mustn't take any notice of this," she said looking at Winter. "She's not herself. She's been unwell. I'm afraid I hadn't understood how unwell. Hush, my dear, do. Don't judge her by this, Superintendent. She's a very good, kind teacher. I have every faith in her." She looked up at Winter valiantly.

"I'm not at all sure she ought to be in charge of children," said Winter.

"Don't judge her by this, I ask you. She's been ill."

"Horrid, beastly, lying child," sobbed Miss Peterson.

"I don't think she is lying," said Winter. "There is something hanging over Minny Duveen whatever its source."

The word hospital came through Miss Peterson's muffled sobs.

"Yes," said Winter, "that's obviously our next port of call."

CHAPTER EIGHT

THROUGH ALL THE alarms and anxieties Mrs. Daft continued on her round collecting for the Christmas Club. She was a muddler, and her arithmetic was bad, but she came armed with gossip and news so that she was a welcome figure in most of the houses. Even the woman to whom she had once supplied three walking and talking dolls when she had paid for an electric mixer was glad to see her. The whole neighbourhood was alive with comments and information about the murder. Some of it was well informed and accurate, some of it wildly wrong, but all of it was racy and alert. No tale lost in the telling in this neighbourhood.

"I hear they've put that man Winter on the case," said the woman who had once received the three dolls. She and Mrs. Daft were sitting, in a companionable way, over a bottle of Guinness and a plate of ham sandwiches, in a well-heated and bright kitchen. The son of the house was a decorator and he had done the kitchen over in the style he called 'contemporary'. Mrs. Daft complained that having every wall a different colour and the ceiling bright blue made her dizzy, but his mother was proud of it. "And it didn't cost me a penny," she said. "For it's all left-overs."

"I hear they've put Winter on it," she said again. "Oh he's a one. He'll do it."

"It's to be hoped he knows what he's doing," said Mrs. Daft as if she doubted. "But one thing's sure: he's not what I'd call a good-tempered man."

Mrs. Daft had suffered particularly from the Superintendent's critical and watchful eye. She felt that he noticed her in all her employments such as the dusting at No. 5, the polishing at No. 3 and what she called her 'good do over' at No. 2. A number of the little perquisites such as the traditional bowl of dripping and the left-over cold meat, and the less usual half-finished boxes of chocolates and the almost empty boxes of cigarettes which she was accustomed to stow quietly away in her big bag had to be forgone this week.

"They say he never lets go," said his admirer. "Relentless Winter, they call him."

"Not what I call him," said Mrs. Daft. "And not what those boys of his who have to work with him call him either, from all I hear. And I don't blame them. The way he treats them isn't right in a democratic country. And then he's always following me around. I don't like it."

"And how's your daughter, my dear?" said her friend to change the subject.

"No better and no worse," was the dour reply.

"Oh, the poor love. Still I'm sure she will be better."

"I'm sure I don't know why we have children," said Mrs. Daft looking down into her glass of Guinness. "Look at poor old Booth, gasping his life away in hospital because the police frightened him so with their silly questions that they brought on a heart attack as anyone could have told them would be the case. His mother didn't bring him into the world for that. I don't know; it's painful getting born and it's painful dying. It's hard on mothers."

"Indeed it is, dear," said her friend, meanwhile measuring the liquid left in the bottle with a skilful eye. "Still we have a lot to be thankful for with modern science." She poured out the drink with a calculated fairness.

"*I* haven't," said Mrs. Daft.

"No, dear, all right," said her friend, seeing that she was not to be cheered up. She noticed the speed at which the food and drink were disappearing. "Well there's one thing, thank goodness, you've kept your digestion. Cheer up, dear, we'll see you a granny yet."

Mrs. Daft finished her mouthful and rose. "I'm off now," she said. "Got to pop into one or two other places. Tootle-oo."

"And one of those places will be the Victory," said her friend to herself as she watched the fat black-clad figure toddle off. "I wouldn't like to say it aloud, but I think Doris is overdoing the drink. That Guinness wasn't her first tonight, by a long way." She looked regretfully at the empty bottle, then she popped it tidily behind the sofa in the window. "Well she can stand treat next week. Fair's fair between friends, and she must have a nice tidy sum tucked away somewhere, must Doris, after all these years. No one can say she's spent her money on her back," she said, stroking her own good strong satin blouse, "for I've known that coat for twenty years, and it wasn't new then."

It was Mrs. Daft's habit to trot to the Victory at the end of her evening's work and there to do her accounts. She sat thumbing over her grubby book and making notes with a well-licked stub of pencil. She kept the actual cash in a little leather bag.

"Someone will follow the old girl one night and do her in for that bag of money," the barmaid would complain in a worried way. "There'll be murder done."

Indeed Mrs. Daft herself used to look nervously around her and once or twice she complained that someone was following her, but all the same she kept up the habit and drank her stout and did her accounts with pretty equal enthusiasm every collecting day. The collecting day itself varied, sometimes there were as many as three in a week and sometimes none for a month. It depended how she felt.

She trotted into the Victory as usual, and sat down, dropping her bag with a thud on the table.

"You've had a good night, Ma," said the barmaid, mentally assessing the weight of the bag; she poured out Mrs. Daft's usual stout.

"Now what about treating yourself to a nice little permanently pleated nylon nightgown for Christmas," suggested Mrs. Daft genially. "Only twenty-nine and six."

"Oh, too cold for me," said the barmaid with a mock shiver. "I'm strictly a wool and long-sleeved nightgown girl."

"What, a nice young lovebird like you?" said Mrs. Daft sceptically.

The girl looked at Mrs. Daft doubtfully; there was more in her than met the eye. You never knew quite what to expect from the old thing. Not always what you got from her certainly. What with her and old Booth around! thought the girl.

Mrs. Daft turned back to her account book, over which she pored with concentration and a good deal of licking of fingers as she turned over the pages.

"I hear they had the police at St. Clare's Hospital today," said the barmaid, making conversation. "We've had a good deal of extra custom since the murder you know, journalists and so on, and of course they know they can talk freely in front of me, I'm always ever so discreet, so one way and another I hear a good deal of talk the public don't hear."

"Yes, you're so discreet," said Mrs. Daft. "That's why you're known as the eyes and ears of Chelsea."

"Oh, you rude old thing," said the girl.

Mrs. Daft gave a hoarse laugh and returned to her counting out of the little piles of coppers and silver.

"Mad," said the barmaid, not inaudibly, but all the same not with too much spirit. She had had encounters with Mrs. Daft before and had not always come off the better.

"What about the hospital then?" said Mrs. Daft.

The barmaid was torn between a desire to show off her undoubted knowledge of what had gone on when Coffin and Winter visited the hospital, and an equally strong desire to snub Mrs. Daft. Her burden of knowledge won.

"They came in and said, 'We're the police, we're in a hurry and we want to interview the people who worked with Dr. O'Finney as soon as possible'," said the barmaid.

"That'd be Winter," observed Mrs. Daft. "Oh, he's a polite boy. I can see why he went into the Force. He was looking out for the truncheon."

"They had a job getting everyone lined up though, all the same," went on the girl. "Well, you know what they are like in hospitals, always shoving you on to the next bench to sit for an hour. They say Winter was in a real temper in no time."

"Ah," said Mrs. Daft.

"Then it all came out."

"What did?" asked Mrs. Daft in a sharp voice. She popped her money into her leather bag, drew the strings tight and leaned forward expectantly, one dirty, strong little hand grasping her drink.

A crowd of people pushed through the bar and the girl reluctantly turned her attention to them, but making mysterious nods to Mrs. Daft as she did so.

"What's come over the girl?" muttered the old lady irritably. "Who does she think she is? Why can't she keep to the subject?"

"Oh, go on," said Mrs. Daft as soon as the girl came near her again. "Tell me *what* came out."

"Oh, hush, can't you?" asked the girl indignantly. "Can't you see it's them?"

Mrs. Daft looked over her shoulder. She saw Sergeant Coffin who was wearing a bright check tweed suit and a yellow tie. Compared with Winter in his sombre attire, he looked as though he was in fancy dress.

"Just come from the Pantomine?" she asked cocking a knowledgeable old eye at his clothes.

"Too early in the season, ma'am."

"I see you've got the Demon King with you, though," she went on with a look at Winter. She looked again at Coffin. "Now I know what they mean by a plain-clothes detective." She began to giggle.

"Don't take any notice of the old thing," said the barmaid leaning forward hastily. "She's a bit queer today. I think it's lovely tweed you've got on. Shouldn't mind a bit of it myself."

"Even policemen don't have to wear dark clothes all the time and as we had to make a trip into the country today I thought I'd wear my tweeds."

"Yes," said Winter.

"It must have been very deep country," said the barmaid looking at Coffin more closely.

"Yes," said Winter again.

"And what about little Sir Echo," chirped Mrs. Daft remorselessly from her table. "Did he go too?"

"Don't take any notice," whispered the barmaid. "I think she's trying to annoy you. I heard all about you today," she went on. "How you went to the hospital and how it all came out that the last thing the doctor said at the hospital was that he was going to murder someone."

"And not the first," said Mrs. Daft. "And not the first."

They ignored her. "Well, you've picked up the information as usual," said Coffin admiringly.

"And what brings you down these parts now? Just a nice cosy drink?" She smiled sweetly. It never did any harm to be in with the police.

Winter answered for them both. "No," he said sombrely. "I came this way to see *you*."

The girl knocked over a glass.

"You've got some information I want."

The two policemen were at the end of a long and exacting day. The Hospital of St. Clare and St. Mark had proved to be an institution that even Superintendent Winter found baffling. Never in his life had he been left to wait on so cold a chair, conducted down longer and longer corridors and steeper flights of stairs, knocked on more doors only to find that the person he wanted was not there after all. And the smell of hospital had given him a headache. At the end of the day he was an exhausted and anxious man. What he had learnt at the hospital hung over him in a threatening cloud. And he was not an imaginative man.

The Hospital of St. Clare had been founded in the eleventh century by a pious Anglo-Norman landlord for the sick watermen of the Thames. He had been to Rome on a pilgrimage and had been most impressed by a hospital there and he had thought it would be a good idea to secure his own salvation by endowing a similar institution at home. He placed his hospital on the banks of the Thames where he had a spare piece of land. It had survived and flourished over the centuries and was now a great rambling series of buildings dealing with every type of ailment, hardly any of which would have been recognised by the original founder. In addition it housed three important research units to one of which Jack O'Finney was attached.

Like all institutions which have survived and flourished over the centuries the Hospital took its own authority very seriously and anyone else's very lightly. Superintendent Winter found that *his* authority just bounced off the side. The hospital may just have heard of Scotland Yard—that other building overlooking the river—but it had never heard of him.

And as luck would have it the Administrator of the

hospital was a man called Spring. "If Winter comes can Spring be far behind," was the joke which soon preceded him round the hospital.

"I'm looking for Dr. Green," Winter found himself repeating before a succession of thoughtful faces. "He worked a good deal with Dr. O'Finney, whose death I am investigating. You know he's dead, I suppose," he added bitterly.

"Oh, yes, we know that," they admitted, "but this is a big hospital, and Dr. Green is not easy to find."

The superintendent came to the conclusion that doctors spend a large part of their day walking about. "Worse than being on the Force," Sergeant Coffin agreed in a mutter. Another large part of a doctor's day was apparently made up of having low-voiced conversations which looked serious and anxious, but when overheard often turned out to be about last night's party or the latest medical indiscretion of one of the consultants.

In the end they tracked down Dr. Green. He was a large fair man in his early thirties, already going bald and wearing his white coat like a sack. He had, of course, already been questioned by a detective constable who had asked him the sort of routine questions a murdered man's associates do get asked. But Winter and his satellite had come with a special question in mind.

The interview took place in a small research laboratory; the walls were lined with cages containing bright-eyed white rats under large glass covers rather like the sort of cake and sandwich container seen in old-fashioned railway buffets.

"You have to be careful to keep the sexes apart," said Dr. Green seeing the two men look curiously at his rats and mice. "Or they fight like fiends. Look nice peaceful little animals don't they? Eat each other as soon as look at you. Sooner." He seemed a laconic man with a decided mind.

"I used to keep white mice once," said Coffin.

"Decent little beasts really. Not got the spirit of the rat though. God, you should see the fight they put up. Sometimes they *won't* die."

"I suppose you get used to it and take it all in your stride," said Coffin regretfully.

"No, well, no," said Dr. Green, hesitating for the first time. "You never really do that somehow. But what I'm doing is necessary work."

"And Dr. O'Finney's work, that too was valuable?"

"Yes," said Dr. Green a trifle sadly. "Potentially I should say it was very valuable indeed." He took a white rat out of a cage, looked it intently in the face, and then put it back. "Success, if he had achieved it, and now I suppose someone else will carry on his work, will save the lives of hundreds, perhaps thousands, of children each year."

"He cared for children?"

"Yes, you know he did. It wasn't entirely scientific curiosity with him, although there was that too. I've seen him bitterly regretful when a child he has been delivering has been born dead—he was a fine obstetrician you know—or, as once happened here, the child was terribly malformed, a monstrous idiot. We had a doctor here once who was not good with children, he was well-meaning but clumsy. He could hurt a child and frighten it without the least intending to do either. Jack was in a fury with him. 'I could kill that man for making a child suffer,' he said to me. He had violence in him, had Jack," and the doctor fell silent.

"Violence calls out violence," said Coffin. He was thinking of the two young men who had lived with Jack, and wondering if either of them had killed him.

"But you know," said Dr. Green, "I worked with him but we weren't specially friendly. I'm married and a home man and Jack," he grinned, "was very much unmarried, wasn't he? We didn't have a lot in common, although we liked each other. His real friend here, and don't misunderstand me, was Sister Antrobus."

Winter raised his eyebrows.

"She was half French, you see, and I've always thought Jack had some foreign blood in him. They were just friends you know, talked French together, and I dare say Jack gave her a kiss or two occasionally, he couldn't keep that out of any relationship, but basically they were just two fellow-countrymen in an alien land. That's a funny thing for me to have said," he added puzzled. "Still now I think about it, it's just how I felt about Jack. Anyway, she would know about him I think."

"Yes, we'd better see Sister Antrobus."

"She's on leave," said Dr. Green. "Anyway, I haven't seen her around."

Sister Mary Antrobus, when she was finally discovered at her little house in Sussex, showed herself to be a large, robust, handsome young woman with a graceful walk. It was not difficult to see that she could be an attractive companion. She was in her garden setting out bulbs for the winter. She set down her trowel, took off her big gardening gloves and faced them frankly.

She admitted she was half French and had been a great friend of Dr. O'Finney's. They had met while she was in charge of the nursery at St. Clare's.

"Yes," she said, "he did make that remark about killing a man if he harmed a child. I think he could have done it on sufficient provocation. He did so love children. He had some soreness about it, too. Something must have happened to him once. But even to me he never said anything, although I think he knew he could speak freely."

"He was half French wasn't he?" said Winter guessing.

"Oh, no, not half French at all."

"Funny," said Winter disappointed, "I'd got the impression he was. So he was wholly Irish was he?"

"No," she said with a half smile, "he wasn't wholly Irish, not Irish at all. He'd never been in Ireland and he hadn't a drop of Irish blood in his veins."

"What?"

"I know what you are going to say: His name. But it wasn't his name at all. He was called Janos Filipec, or he had been called that. He changed it when he was naturalised. He had a British passport and his medical degrees were London but by birth he was a Hungarian and he had lived nearly all his life in Paris until 1945. I suppose he half pretended to be an Irishman because the Irish and the Hungarians are so very alike."

"Paris did you say?"

"Yes, Paris. If you want to find out more about Jack O'Finney you ought to go to Paris. He still had a relation or two there. Not many though," she added grimly. "Not so very many survived the war years. He had a bad time himself and he was only a boy then. He wasn't so old," she said sadly, "when he died."

"There was more than friendship on her side anyway," thought Coffin with pity.

"Do you know the address of his relations there?"

She shook her head. "But wait a minute. The last time he came back I remember he brought me some gloves. I have such big hands you see," and she looked at them ruefully, "they need French gloves to look graceful, and at the same time he brought back a bottle of scent for the barmaid at the Victory. He'd promised her, and I remember he laughed and said that he'd almost forgotten but remembered at the last minute because he was staying in a house next to a scent shop, you know, one of those lovely shops you only get in France where they sell nothing but scent. There might be the address of the shop pasted on the bottle, they do that quite often. She may not still have the bottle, of course."

She had something else on her mind that she wanted to tell them.

"You know, Jack said something to me once that I've been worrying over. Maybe there's nothing in it, but it might be connected with his murder." She paused. "I think I'd better tell you."

"Yes, you certainly must."

"He was talking about people he knew; I'll repeat what he said. He said: 'I've certainly got a mad one on my hands, that one thinks there's a man circling round on the moon watching!'"

"Someone with a persecution mania," said Coffin, watching her.

"Someone with schizophrenia, is what it sounds like," said the knowledgeable nurse. "And they can be dangerous."

Back in the Victory the barmaid produced a bottle of Chanel No. 5 from behind a row of whisky bottles.

J. Brabant. Parfumier. No. 8 Rue de la Roche, Avénue de l'Opéra. Paris.

"Paris," said the superintendent. "And I was going to the seaside this week-end."

"Oh, well," said Coffin. "I could go if you liked."

"No," said Winter austerely. "Business before pleasure. I shall take the night ferry."

CHAPTER NINE

SUPERINTENDENT WINTER DEPARTED for Paris. He was wearing his best overcoat and a pink carnation tucked into his buttonhole. He left plenty of instructions behind.

"I wonder what he thinks I'm going to do when he's gone," grumbled Coffin. "Put my feet up and have a nice cup of tea?" He telephoned his mother. "Take off the haddock you're cooking for my supper, Mum, I won't be home." Her voice crackled over the wire:

"It wasn't a haddock, Sammy boy, but a nice bit of cod."

Her son turned back to the type-written instructions his chief had left behind him. It was not so much what Winter had asked him to do as what he had asked him not to do that annoyed the sergeant.

Do not take any more interviews with the suspected persons in Pontifex Passage: I want them left strictly alone. "To simmer I suppose," said Coffin.

Do not let them see too much of you; I sometimes think you get too familiar with the suspects; this may be your technique: it is not mine. "Knock them down and don't say sorry, that's more your technique," observed Coffin.

Do get hold of the Medical Examiner and make him give you the detailed report on Dr. O'Finney. Why has it been such a long time?

Do remember to check all possible statements at all possible points. I have reminded you of this before. I wouldn't like to call you credulous, but let's say that for a policeman you are over-trustful. "Not your trouble anyway, old boy," said Coffin.

The superintendent had had a last thought: Do not take the official car if you can walk or go by bus.

Coffin put the paper down crossly.

At the end of his first day alone he had managed to blast his way through all the commandments of his superior officer. "Not that I did it on purpose," he told himself modestly. "I saw my opportunity and I took it."

His first opportunity had come when having trudged wearily round London on a variety of errands connected with the twin problems of Minny Duveen and Jack O'Finney, he turned into the Picasso Espresso Bar not far from his Divisional Headquarters. It was also not far from Pontifex Passage, so it was not surprising really to see it so full of familiar faces.

He could see Perdita and Fanny, the latter wearing what was obviously a new smart suit of thick tailored silk. Tom and Berry were there too, watching Fanny who was studying her face anxiously in a pocket mirror.

"There's a new wrinkle," she said. "Oh, you've no idea how worrying it is to have your face as your fortune. I'm living on capital."

"Live on mine," offered Berry generously.

"So I would, dear, if you had any," said Fanny dolefully.

Coffin sat down near them and ordered his cup of coffee.

"Time was when a cup of coffee meant a nice hot drink full of milk and sugar," he said, "and not this bitter lukewarm hemlock."

"I'm not sure hemlock would be so bitter," said Tom seriously. "It was mixed with opium for Socrates."

"I could just do with a nice bowl of opium," said Coffin.

"No, not really you couldn't," said Fanny leaning forward and patting his hand. "Opium is nasty stuff. Unless you are brought up on it like the Chinese; and you couldn't have been."

"No, the old Mum didn't know much about diet, but she spared me that. A drop of gin would have been more her idea of devilment."

"How do you know so much about opium?" asked Perdita.

"Oh, a girl friend of mine told me all about it. She's been in India. She's just married a Parsee."

"I didn't know you could."

"Of course. If you're a Parsee too."

"But is she?"

"Well, she's one now. He's so nice. He's a *fair* Parsee."

"Goodness, are there any?"

"Oh yes, he's a *very* fair Parsee."

"I'm so glad. Are they happy."

"I expect so. You know it's the religion where when you die they lay your body out on the mountain side and the vultures open it and pick your bones."

"What a lot she's got to look forward to, your friend," said Perdita. "Not very cosy though."

"It's very hygienic."

"Oh, surely not," said Berry, who together with Tom and Coffin, had been listening to this conversation with rapt attention. "Surely not. That's the sort of jargon people pick up, like saying things are 'natural'. That usually means something unpleasant. Give me art every time."

Fanny was hurt. "Well, don't snub me, Berry. You are cross today. You weren't a bit interested in what I told you about my new dress."

"Not cross, Fanny. Just worried. There seems plenty to worry about at the moment."

"Yes, just look at it all," said Perdita egged on in spite of her better judgement to a stupid rashness by the presence of the detective. Coffin wanted to shout to her "Stop, stop, listen to what you are saying," but he knew he must let her go on. "There's Jack dead, Mr. Booth dying, and my mother and Minny—well the less said about that the better perhaps." She showed every sign however of saying a good deal more about it.

This was perhaps why Tom leaned forward and spoke to Coffin. "We're not really at the end of this case are we? Go on, say, you ought to know."

"I don't know," said Coffin helplessly. They're interviewing me now, he thought. Not what the old man ordered. "I might as well tell you in confidence that we are beginning to have an idea that the person behind it all is mad."

"Oh, well, if it's a mad person you'll get on to them soon won't you? After all they will give themselves away." Perdita was very pale.

"Yes," said Coffin. "Perhaps. But what about the lunatic fringe? The dotty, the half crazy, the almost sane. What about them, all free to walk the streets of London?"

"There's no doubt whatever," said Berry solemnly, "that eugenics ought to be taken seriously. Sterilisation and all that. There'd be less of this physical and mental ill health if it were so."

Fanny stretched her limbs; she was conscious that she was healthy.

"Why do we let the poor stock, the stupid, the crazy, go on perpetuating themselves?"

"Don't be shrill," said Fanny. "You and Jack were always going on about eugenics."

"You're frightening me," said Perdita. She took Tom's hand in hers. She felt impelled to rush on with her confession. "If you're looking for someone just a little crazy perhaps you ought to consider me."

"Shut up, Perdita," said Tom.

"Well, I have to admit that my chances of sanity are not high," said Perdita gabbling on. "That's what happened to my father, you know. Oh, no one talks about it, and he's dead now, poor love, but he did go mad, quite, quite dotty and perhaps a little violent. I could inherit it. Only I do hope I haven't," she said bursting into tears. "Poor little Minny, I really wouldn't harm her, and it would be so terrible for Mother, she's had it all once, she nearly went mad herself, poor darling."

"She's not mad," said Tom fiercely over her head to the sergeant. "Of course she isn't."

"Oh, Perdita," said Fanny hastening forward with her comfort. She had her own worries but she couldn't see Perdita like this. "If you really are mad you don't know."

"Don't you," said Perdita, still weeping. "Like being dead?"

They looked at each other helplessly.

"Here," said Coffin. "I'll order a car and get you home." The superintendent's last order thus went by the board. "Take the weight off my feet too," he added with a gleam of mirth.

"I don't want to go home," said Perdita. "I don't want to go home to Mother."

But they ignored this and the sergeant got the car and took the whole party off in it. In deference to Perdita's request he let her and Fanny out at Fanny's little flat.

"Only a man could have killed Jack O'Finney," he said in a quiet voice to Perdita, then he had himself driven home to the rooms above Hammersmith Broadway. The smell of fish was still very strong and he sniffed at it morosely.

"Well, that's that for today," he said, as he took off his shoes and socks. "I hope it's raining in Paris."

It was indeed raining in Paris. Superintendent Winter was not enjoying himself. His best overcoat was damp and his carnation was wilting.

He consulted his map. Go to the nearest metro station, he told himself, ask for the Place de l'Opéra, get out there, then turn left. But of course he had no idea where the nearest metro station was. He considered taking a taxi, but frugally decided against this. Also, he was just a little frightened of the taxi drivers.

He chose a mild-looking passer-by and went up.

"*Avez-vous——?*" he began.

The man shook his head.

"*Avez-vous——?*" he began again.

"No," said the man.

"You didn't let me finish," said Winter.

"Wouldn't have done you any good if I did. I'm English."

The superintendent saw then that he was standing just by a metro station so he went down. He was almost swept over just near the bottom of the stairs by a sudden great surge of people who rushed past him shouting. He politely stood aside to let them pass. When he got to the bottom he discovered the reason for the rush. A train had just come in and although the crowd that had just rushed past him was safely aboard he himself was barred even from the platform by an iron grille.

After a twenty-minute wait another wave of shouting people hurled themselves down the stairs so he knew a train was due and joined in the rush. He found his umbrella a help.

The train was very full; only a little pull-down seat at the end of the carriage was empty. He pulled it down and sat on it. He sat for ten minutes and then began to have an uncomfortable feeling that he was being stared at.

"Know I'm English," he thought and tried to forget it.

"*Espèce de polichinelle, va!*" said an old woman with a titter.

Winter thought for a moment; these words had not been included in his vocabulary at the Berlitz school but after all he had not been in the Force for thirty years without becoming something of an expert on words of abuse. He recognised the tone if not the language.

He looked around; his companions on the pull-down seats were three ladies and a man without legs.

Slowly he raised his eyes to the lettering above the seats which informed him that the seats were reserved for pregnant women and veterans of the Republic.

"Very French," he thought as he rose, trying not to look embarrassed. The *Daily Telegraph* for yesterday slipped from his arm.

"English," the old woman across the way informed the carriage. The atmosphere relaxed. But not Winter.

"Scots, madam," he corrected coldly. It was a part of his saga that he had not so far told to the waiting world. And it was true in a way; his mother had been born in Aberdeen, although of English parents who were on holiday there. Like most Londoners Winter was very anxious to prove he was really something else.

"*C'est égal.*"

"That depends, madam," said Winter even more coldly, "which side of the border you are."

He leapt to his feet as his station flashed into view. The door was jammed with people getting on and it was only just as the train started to move again that he succeeded in pushing his way to the front and staggering on to the platform.

A voice hailed him from the train.

"Here you are, Scotsman," called the old lady, and she threw his umbrella after him.

Winter was surprised to discover himself in the Rue de la Roche with comparative ease. The rain had stopped and a misty yellow sun was shining on the wet gutters. The Rue de la Roche was a narrow grey cobbled street lined with tall but thin houses. Winter walked slowly up it looking for J. Brabant, Parfumier. He found the shop quite easily. It stood in the middle of the street with a hotel called Hotel Sainte-Beuve on one side and a private house on the other. Winter had to decide which to try first. He chose the house.

It was a house of dark grey stone, well shuttered, and apparently completely empty.

"If it's anything like the houses in Bayswater," said Winter thoughtfully, "someone will be having a look out of a window all the same."

He rang the bell. He could hear it jangling away in the distance. No one answered. He rang again. There was still no answer. He was considering resentfully whether he should ring again when he heard a distant shuffling.

He waited patiently for some minutes, then realised that the shuffling had stopped. He leant down and peered through the keyhole; it was a very large keyhole with a strong cold draught blowing through it. Nor could he see very far.

After a while he realised, considerably disconcerted, that he was staring into a watering grey eye which was looking out at him. He raised himself smartly and gave a long tug at the door. Almost at once the door was opened.

From what he had seen through the keyhole and from the slow approach of the slippered feet he had expected to find an old woman looking at him. What he saw was a little girl of about eight or so; she was dressed in a grubby blue dress and had worn, run-down slippers on her feet. Both her eyes and her nose were running.

In his careful French Winter had prepared himself to say that he was a British police officer and that he was looking for a Jack O'Finney who might be known here under the name of Janos Filipec, but the words died on his lips. He considered asking her to get her mother but even this seemed stupid.

Doesn't look as though she's *got* a mother, he said to himself.

The child looked at him doubtfully and cautiously, then muttered something to herself. Then she began to close the door.

Winter frowned. It was not possible to question a child. He looked at her again. There was a curious appearance of age about this child, she was young and yet she was not young. She was childish but hardly childlike. He began to wonder if she was a dwarf. She was tiny but you could not call her stunted.

"I'm not a child lover, I know," he said to himself, "but you're not a very attractive child, my dear."

The door was now shut firmly in his face, so he made for the hotel.

The outside of the Hotel Sainte-Beuve was dowdy and in need of painting and faintly depressing, but inside, to Winter's surprise, there was an air of comfort approaching luxury. The lobby was covered with a fitted grey carpet and there was a white and gold staircase with flowers and plants and palm trees to be seen in the distance behind thick glass doors.

"Can't quite see Jack O'Finney here, or can I?" he

said. "He certainly did seem to have money from somewhere so perhaps he did stay here."

He tucked his umbrella under his arm and approached the desk which was in one corner of the room with a large mirror behind it, the purpose of which was not lost on the experienced Winter.

'They've got some clients they don't trust then in this smart place,' he decided, much cheered by the thought. He felt more at home.

"Good evening, monsieur," said a young man as he got near the desk. He spoke in English and Winter, although regretful that he looked so English (that a good police officer should sink into his background was one of the maxims he handed over to his subordinates) was grateful that the conversation was conducted in English.

At once he asked if a Mr. O'Finney had stayed in this hotel. The young man consulted his books and declared very soon that he had not.

"Janos Filipec then," said Winter.

"If he was the type to have two names, monsieur, then he is hardly likely to come *here*."

"No?" said Winter letting his eye travel to the mirror. "Really? Well, it wasn't an alias and he wasn't, as far as I know, a man with a criminal record, he simply changed his name when he became a naturalised British subject and that is common enough. So look again will you, please?"

There was still no result and the young man closed his book, not unpleased. Winter sighed. He was used to dead ends, every police officer was, but he did not enjoy them.

"He used to live in this district, I think. A good many years ago. Say during the war."

The young man shrugged. "I will get Madame," he announced. He disappeared behind the glass doors and presently reappeared with a stout middle-aged woman. She gave Winter a quick appraising glance. "Nonsense, of course he is indeed a British police officer, you have only to look at him," Winter heard her say. She came over to him, the expression on her face nicely judged between a smile and a frown.

She shook her head as Winter explained once more what he wanted. Neither of the names he offered seemed to mean anything to her.

"If he was a refugee, a *déraciné* Hungarian, as you seem to suggest, he is not likely to have lived in *this* street," she said dryly.

Winter raised his eyebrows.

"But you are English," she said, "I forget, you would not understand. Around the corner from here was one of the local headquarters of the Gestapo. Oh, *they* were gentry. Yes, and we had Dr. Pétiot, the mass murderer, not so far away. It was not a good district for those who wanted to go on living."

"But he was only a little boy then."

She shrugged. "And would that have made any difference?"

"After the war," Winter went on, "this boy came to England and was educated and became a doctor, or so I believe. An obstetrician and a gynaecologist. Does that mean anything to you?"

"Little Jakko," she said. "Who would have thought it." She laughed. "But of course I know *him*. He worked here in this hotel as boot-boy, then he was a messenger for a firm on the Bourse. They took an interest in him there, because of his history and because he was clever. Then a patron took him up and sent him to London to get educated. Ah well, he deserved good fortune, poor boy," she sighed. "He came back here often to visit his sister."

"His sister?"

"Oh, yes, she continues to live next door. Sixteen years or so now, it will be. It is surprising you missed her. She hardly ever goes out. You couldn't expect it."

"I called there," said Winter puzzled. "There was no one at home. But I saw the sister's own child, I suppose, her daughter."

"Her daughter?" repeated the woman with a strange look. "She has no daughter. It was the sister you saw."

There was a pause. "But that's impossible," said Winter. "This was a child, the other must be at least a young woman." But even as he spoke he remembered that there had been something very odd about the child.

"If you go back now you may find Mademoiselle Brigitte and her companion, Madame Mouris, at home," suggested the proprietress of the hotel equably. "It's a lodging-house, you know. I dare say Madame was at the market." She had recovered her self-possession but plainly no more information was coming his way.

For a moment he missed Coffin, who would undoubtedly have bounced and joked her into giving more help. "Does Madame Mouris speak English?" he asked.

"No," Madame laughed.

"Then will you perhaps come with me? As a great

favour?" Seeing her look of indecision he added. "Your friend Jakko is dead; he has been killed."

"Poor soul," she said heavily, and for a moment he thought she meant Jack O'Finney, but she went on, "What will she do now?"

Madame Mouris when she at last appeared was very like the little grey mouse the euphony of her name suggested. In her way she was a smart little mouse with bright, brisk eyes and well covered little paws. Her lodging-house, too, once you were past its sober exterior and the disconcerting impression given by Mademoiselle Brigitte, was clearly a lodging-house of character and distinction. The furniture and decorations were dark and sombre but at the same time rich and gleaming.

As soon as she understood Winter's errand Madame Mouris was willing enough to talk, but she did so in a rapid French which Madame the Proprietress, now mysteriously in charge of the whole proceedings, translated for Winter's benefit.

Madame Mouris talked at the same time of course. "The poor child, it is going to be difficult to explain it all to the child. We call her the child," she said to Winter who could understand this much, "although heaven knows she's hardly a child in years." She directed her speech to her neighbour, "Does he know about her? How it all happened?"

Madame from the Hotel Sainte-Beuve shook her head.

"Poor little Brigitte," said Madame Mouris mournfully. "Oh, well, she will be looked after. We might take her to Lourdes. Sister Françoise Angélique suggested Lourdes herself."

"It will take more than Lourdes to make much difference to poor Brigitte," said Madame, the proprietress, briskly; she was clearly anti-clerical. "It is fourteen years too late for prayers, Marie."

Between them they told the story. In the last years of the war, just before France was liberated, Jakko and his sister had lived in the Rue de la Roche with Madame Mouris who was a remote kinswoman by marriage and who had made herself responsible for them when their parents had 'disappeared', a disappearance which was no mystery sadly enough but which was better not inquired into for the children's sake. Madame Mouris had sheltered the children successfully until the confused months when Paris was struggling to free herself before the approach of the Allied armies. Jakko was about thirteen and his sister about eight years old. One day she had gone out to play in the streets, a habit discouraged by Madame Mouris but not altogether prevented.

Madame Mouris began to cry. "It was my fault. I should have been stricter. More firm with her about not leaving the house."

"You cannot blame yourself, Marie," said Madame patting her on the back. "You did everything you could. The child was away ten hours, Monsieur. Then she was—returned on the doorstep, she was unconscious and quite naked, wrapped in a blanket. Afterwards," she shook her head. "Well, you can see her now, she has never altered."

"But could it possibly happen?"

"You see that it *has* happened. There is the proof." Madame shook her head. "A shock to the whole system, to the glands, in particular the thyroid glands, the doctors say to us 'it could be so' but we *know* that it was."

"And you never found out what happened?"

"It was a bad time for finding out things. We never found out. The child could tell us nothing. We could only guess. The Gestapo had an office round the corner. They were nice young bloods there," she said grimly.

"We don't really know," said Madame Mouris, still dribbling tears. "I blame myself."

Jakko had taken the disaster badly and yet in a way it had moulded his character.

"Before he was an idle young lad, afterwards he was harder, older, bitter to all except children whom he loved for Brigitte's sake. He worked hard to be a success and well, you know all about that. And now he too is dead," said Madame Mouris with a sigh. "Ah well, they were a doomed family."

"Well, that's enough, Marie," said her friend briskly. "Not too much gloom, eh, Detective?"

"And Dr. O'Finney came back often to see his sister?" asked Winter. "You don't mind me calling him by that name? It's how I always think of him."

"Oh, he came back often and always with new ideas about treatment for her but none of it worked as you can see, although she's a dear girl. I knew as soon as you started asking questions who you wanted, but of course I wasn't going to answer until I could see you meant him and her no harm. You can see that?"

"Yes," answered Winter.

"And then of course he had business over here," put

in Madame Mouris who had been pursuing her own thoughts.

"Had he indeed?" said Winter pricking up his ears. "What sort of business?"

Madame Mouris looked embarrassed; she had said too much and she knew it.

"Well, I shall be going, Marie," said her friend underlining this impression by the celerity with which she departed.

Winter sat down on one of the hard chairs which Madame Mouris kept in her private back sitting-room. She stood opposite him nervously. For the first time since he had stepped in Paris Winter felt that the cards were in his hands.

"Oh, well, I don't think you could really call it business."

"What would you call it?" asked Winter. He was pleased with his French. "Go on," he prompted, "if you wouldn't call it business, what would you call it?"

"Oh, a friendly arrangement. Quite legal he told me, and after all he had lots of expenses with poor Brigitte and if he liked good things, well, he deserved to have them. Mind you I know nothing about it."

In fact she clearly knew a little more than she admitted but not very much. One of her other lodgers, her prize and best lodger, a Charles Lenoir, was a merchant on the Bourse; he and Jack had some business relations.

"I don't know what. Naturally they would not tell me," she asserted blandly. "One woman in business is enough."

For a moment Winter let this pass. "What woman?" he then said.

Madame Mouris shook her head. She did not know the lady's name but she was tall, slim and very handsome. "A very English type," said Madame Mouris admiringly.

"Isobel Duveen," said Winter. "I knew it." But in his moment of triumph he paused to add crossly, "But I wish I knew exactly what they had been up to."

The more information he extracted the more complicated his puzzle became; he knew now far more about Jack O'Finney, he could guess a good deal about Mrs. Duveen, but he was as far as ever from knowing who was the murderer.

He knew now, however, that it was not a simple case of Jack being killed in a quarrel.

"I wonder what Coffin's got hold of while I have been away?" he asked himself.

He travelled back by the night ferry, his second night of travelling, the carnation was very drooping by now, and went straight to work. He went to the head of the Frauds Department, an old friend and enemy.

"What you again?" said that gentleman. "Got any more jewel smugglers for me?" This was a reference to Winter's almost accidental capture of a trio of smugglers while he was investigating a murder at Bow-on-Sea. "I should think all the smart alecs and con men start to run when they see you coming now."

"I want help from you this time instead of doing your job for you. Mind, I'm not sure if anything illegal's going on, but it's something not quite straightforward and something highly profitable, too."

He told all the relevant facts that he knew. The other

man listened in complete silence and then began to whistle tunelessly.

"The names don't mean anything to me."

"They're up to something, I'm sure."

"Well, none's a better judge of that than you, Winter boy." He rubbed his chin. "Wait a minute. Duveen, did you say? He's a lawyer, isn't he? And *she's* been going round a bit with Christopher Cobley, the new boy on the Parliamentary and Treasury Combined Committee."

"Oh, I dare say."

"And they've been going to considerable trouble to keep the affair, if it is one, under cover."

"You can understand that."

"Oh, no, they're overdoing it, they could afford to be more casual. As it is they are putting red lights out. They've got something on their conscience and it isn't adultery." He began to whistle *The Man who broke the bank at Monte Carlo.* "Paris, the chap on the Bourse, and Mr. Cobley on the Treasury Commission. It all adds up. Winter, my boy, they've been speculating in francs. And there's nothing you can charge them with except using confidential information. But if the word got out then two if not three careers would be mud."

"One of them's dead," Winter reminded him. "Murdered."

"There's your motive for murder then."

"Yes," said Winter dryly, "and a sane motive too."

"All murderers are mad, boy," said the head of the Fraud Squad. "Or they'd stick to nice cosy remunerative crime. Who says crime doesn't pay? You and I know better."

The telephone rang.

"It's for you, Winter," he said, handing it over.

Sergeant Coffin was moodily munching away at the fried cod which his mother, with her usual virtuosity, had served up for breakfast.

The telephone rang.

"What?" said Coffin. He pushed his chair away. "Here, Mum, take this stuff away, I've lost my appetite for it. And don't serve it up for my tea." He was putting on his coat as he spoke.

"What is it?" asked Mrs. Coffin coming out of the kitchen carrying a cup of tea. "Another murder?"

Her son was racing down the stairs. "Yes," his voice called back at her. "And it is one of our men this time."

CHAPTER TEN

"HE ALWAYS WAS an unlucky boy," said Coffin as he looked down on the dead constable. John Evelyn lay with his arms outspread and his head on one side. If it had not been for the curious angle at which his head lay he might have been asleep.

"Broke his neck. How the devil was it done?" Winter had arrived by now.

"Blow on the neck. Cracked the Adam's apple," said Coffin briefly. "Done with a stick, the doctors think."

"God knows this case has been rotten to the core all the way through," said Winter bitterly. "Why and how did he have to get himself killed?" he went on, half exasperated and half anguished.

"He didn't do it for fun," observed Coffin.

They were standing in Pontifex Passage under the tree at the corner. On this spot had been found the body of the dead constable early that morning; the discovery had been made by a street cleaner. The plane tree was dropping its leaves and scattering them on and around the body.

A light canvas shelter had been erected over the body, and each end of Pontifex Passage was cordoned off. Beyond the cordon there was already a large crowd of silent and frightened onlookers.

"He was killed late last night, very late they think,"

said Coffin. "He turned in at the Divisional Headquarters at about ten-thirty to report. You remember you'd made him an Aid to the CID, so he was in plain clothes and more or less working on his own. That was the last time he was seen until the sweeper found him this morning at six."

"Someone was waiting for him here."

"Maybe. Or he came across something he shouldn't have done and had to be shut up."

"In either case it's someone local," said Winter, looking down Pontifex Passage.

"Likely enough."

"Likely!" said Winter. "It's dead certain that it's one of this lot here." He gestured towards the Passage.

Coffin did not answer. In theory it was still possible to make out a case against an outsider, an unknown, a Mr. X, but in fact he knew as well as Winter that was not the truth. The sixth sense which all policemen of experience develop told them that the murderer lay within the group of people they had already met.

"Well, do all the usual tests," said Winter in a sad voice; he had liked young Evelyn.

"Right."

"Not that they will get us anywhere."

Once again the sergeant did not answer. It was quite possible that they would not, but on the other hand there was always the chance that something relevant and suggestive might be turned up: he had known it to happen.

"One more thing, my dear fellow," said Winter in an affable voice.

His subordinate listened with foreboding. If there was one mood of Winter's he liked less than any other it was his cheerful man-of-the-world one, and in spite of the gloom cast by the death of the young constable it was noticeable that Winter had come back from Paris very bouncy and pleased with himself. It was also true to say that if Winter was pleased other people were generally not going to be.

"I suppose he's picked up some information that pleases him," he thought.

"Just one more thing," repeated Winter with an air of secret satisfaction. "Look up what you can on Christopher Cobley, and put a man on him will you?"

"And where will I find him?" said Coffin, rather disconcerted. "He's away, isn't he?"

"Well," said Winter, and his satisfaction was by no means secret now. "That's your job really, isn't it? But you might try his own house."

"You're a cool old bird," thought Coffin, "but you might come right out and say what you know."

"There's someone there, you know," said Winter. "I saw a window curtain move. Worth investigating."

"Did you have a good time in Paris?" asked Coffin.

"I didn't go to have a good time," observed Winter with dignity, "but since you ask me, yes, in a way, I did. Information I certainly picked up, although perhaps it was hardly what I expected."

Coffin looked his question.

"You will certainly be hearing all about it," said Winter, "although this is not the place."

At the end of Pontifex Passage where the police had erected a barrier they had to push their way through silent and unfriendly crowds. There was a bad feeling in the air.

An elderly woman touched Coffin's arm.

"He's dead, is he?" she asked.

"You'll hear all about it in time. Did you know him?"

"He *is* dead. He lodged with me," she muttered. Coffin heard her say something about the rent.

"He won't be paying that, mother."

"Pay? Who's talking about paying?" She was still muttering. "I've been overcharging him now for three years, used to add a little bit here and a little bit there. He must have known, but he never said. He was a good boy."

"Yes, he was a good boy," said Coffin sadly and gravely. "He didn't grudge you your few halfpence, mother. Don't let it worry you now."

"But the thing is I could still do with it," said the woman bursting into tears. "And yet I do grieve for him surely."

Coffin patted her arm silently and walked on.

Winter's little office seemed stuffy and airless in the September sun.

"It was raining in Paris," said the superintendent as he opened windows. Then he sat down and began to talk about what he had learnt on his visit there.

As he did so Coffin realised, what he was only too often ready to forget, the quickness of mind, the persistence, the ready endurance of discomfort, which made Winter a formidable police officer. He was difficult to work with but he drove himself the hardest. The Old Man was a joke to many of his colleagues but the joke was on them.

"And really you know," said Coffin to himself as he listened to the superintendent pouring out his story, "it must be as nerve-racking being Winter as knowing Winter."

In Superintendent Winter's past a knot of circumstances, almost unguessed at by him, but stemming from his childhood, had created in him a genuine distaste for crime and the criminal; this was at once his strength and his weakness. The detective, like the anthropologist, should be detached, should be neither disliked nor disliking. Coffin on the other hand seemed to like and sympathise with the criminals he was pursuing, and this too was perhaps due to his background. He and Winter complemented each other. Together they made a good team.

"On the whole," said Winter, "what I learnt in Paris was a shock to me."

Coffin nodded; he understood.

"I learnt something I would rather not have learnt. And I learnt too that Jack O'Finney could never have been a party to the persecuting of the child Minny, if persecution there is."

"I never thought he could."

"I am beginning to believe, however, that he may have been killed because of it."

In Paris, sitting at a café table, eating an omelet and drinking coffee, he had made careful notes. On his sleepless journey home he had written up these notes and now he presented the result of his labours to Sergeant Coffin.

So Coffin sat at his desk by the open window with the noise of London blowing in from below and read through the chronicle of the Filipec family in Paris. It was not a happy story.

"So that was his submerged life.

"You were right about Paris being a worth-while trip," he told Winter.

"And now you'd better hear what the Fraud people think about things."

"How do they come into it?"

"If you can't read speculation and fraud between the lines in that dossier then you'll never make a detective."

"Sometimes that's what I think myself," admitted Coffin.

Winter placed his clean, newly-washed hands with their short square fingers on the table. A strong smell of carbolic floated over to Coffin. Then in a series of short sentences (he never wasted time on long elegant phrases) he put his case to the sergeant.

"Well, I never did, m'dear," said Coffin, taken off his guard and relapsing into the forbidden speech of his boyhood. "And what about the child?"

"My guess is that she discovered something."

"She's only five."

"So we keep saying. We've befogged our minds with it. Five is a grand age for seeing and listening and repeating—like a parrot."

Coffin reflected that even Winter, no lover of children, did not like the implications of all he was saying.

"And so they frightened her into silence," went on Winter.

A look of almost physical pain spread across Coffin's face. "What kind of a world is it where a mother would do that to her own child?" he asked.

"O'Finney wouldn't stand for it you see," said Winter persuasively, "so he was killed by one of the others, either in a quarrel, which seems most likely, or in an accident."

"There's a good deal in that, certainly," said the sergeant with a shiver. "It must have been the man." He still did not want to believe harm of Isobel Duveen.

Winter shrugged. The telephone rang.

"If that's the report on O'Finney's body from the laboratory," he said at once, "then you can send it over straight away." He maintained an irritable war with the Pathological and Scientific departments. The truth was that he really could not bear to think how much of his work was really done by them.

Winter received the medical report, delivered by a young constable, with open hands.

"Useless to me I expect," he muttered disparagingly as he read. Then he stopped and thoughtfully pinched his nose. Coffin looked at him hopefully.

When Winter had finished he handed the report over to the sergeant.

First of all there was a straightforward report on the body. O'Finney had been healthy enough, although at one time in his early life he had suffered from severe malnutrition with resulting damage to the bones, especially of the chest. Coffin knew enough of the family history to be able to pin this down to the years when the boy and his parents were poverty-stricken refugees in Paris. "Pigeon chested," thought Coffin. "Well, he was a pigeon all right." The sergeant was unwittingly echoing the earlier words of Robert Duveen. "I suppose he'd grown to think of himself as the bold one, the chap that was going to do the plucking, but when it came down to it, he was the one that got plucked. Poor fellow, *he* was the pigeon."

The pathologist went on to notice that just before his death the deceased had washed and shaved his face, had a haircut and trimmed his finger-nails. Coffin shook his head sadly at this.

There had been bruises all over him when he died, as though he had been beaten with a stick. His face, neck, arms and legs were bruised and scratched.

Around his ankles and wrists there had been severe congestion of the blood as well as lacerations.

And then Coffin saw that the pathologist had added to this statement a significant comment:

"It looks as though the poor chap was tied up."

In silence Coffin took in the implications of this remark; he was beginning to see that it altered everything.

"Tied up," he said thoughtfully and aloud.

"Don't keep repeating it," said his chief, who was sitting cleaning the dust of Paris from his finger-nails.

"It means he didn't die in a quarrel that suddenly flared up, that there's no possibility that it was an accident, that it was planned, premeditated murder."

"Means more than that," said Winter, still picking away at his nails.

"He wasn't a strong man," said Coffin. "Rather slight in fact."

"Weedy, you might say."

"You wouldn't think a man would have to tie him up to kill him."

"That's it," said Winter putting down his nail-file. "So no man did. It was a woman."

"Mrs. Duveen is not the only woman in the case," said Coffin who thought he could read Winter's mind. "There are others."

"Certainly there are," said Winter agreeably. "Several others."

"And do you think Mrs. Duveen is the mad person the doctor said he had on his hands?"

"Shouldn't be surprised," said Winter even more agreeably.

"Then how did she tie him up?" said Coffin, acutely putting his finger on the crux of the problem.

Isobel and Christopher Cobley were quarrelling, but at least this time they were doing it in public and not tucked away at the back of a church; they had abandoned the pretence of hardly knowing each other. They understood now that the police were investigating their activities, for Madame Mouris had sent an anxious and all too explanatory telegram. Isobel, at first amused, had then become exasperated and was now angry. Also her companion, she thought, was almost certainly drunk. Under pressure their relationship, never very stable, had degenerated completely.

Isobel in anger was sarcastic.

"Profit," she said. "Two thousand pounds odd. That is, I wonder . . . What did *you* make?"

"About the same." Christopher looked round the restaurant for the wine waiter. They were lunching so early today that the place was almost empty. Over the decorated centre table crowded with dishes of cold lobster, green melon, glazed turkey and stuffed duck he could see the face of Poppet Paine. "More or less."

"More, probably," said Isobel with emphasis. "We haven't been exactly straight with each other, and to tell you the truth, I've kept one or two little things from you."

"You might have had us all in prison."

"I dare say." Isobel's tone was indifferent. "I'm beginning to think we deserved it. So there we are—net profit about two thousand each, and the loss? A marriage and a career or two, perhaps." The lightness of her tone was belied by the hard sad expression of her face.

"We don't know yet."

"We can guess, can't we? Anyway, I have told Robert." Isobel was in fact a good deal less resolute and composed than she pretended.

At last the wine waiter approached bearing his long list.

"Champagne, Christopher?" said Isobel brightly; she felt that for once she was living up to the life her mother had designed for her; she was being the gay brittle woman of the world, facing the break-up of her life with a smile and a desire for champagne. She resisted the temptation to burst into loud refreshing tears.

"Whisky."

"That's right, soak!" said Isobel bitterly and unforgivably.

Christopher flushed but said nothing. Then, "Has it struck you, Isobel, that it's not any trifling charge from the Treasury that we may be facing but a trial for murder?"

"Oh, I think about it all the time," said Isobel almost gaily, but she put on more lipstick with a trembling hand. "However, we hadn't really any motive for killing Jack, had we? I've thought about it hard, and it seems to me that they'd have to establish we had a motive."

"We had any number of motives. We could have quarrelled with him, couldn't we? We had, in fact. He was getting, well, squeamish."

Isobel shrugged.

"My God, you're hard." Poor Isobel, in fact, felt more like an unset jelly but she responded to this by lighting a cigarette with what she hoped was a light gesture.

"I didn't kill him though."

"So you say."

"Thank you. So I say." Isobel was unable to resist a few more fatal words. "At one time what I said would have been enough for you."

"That was before I knew you as I do now." Christopher mopped his forehead. Every time he looked round the room he met Poppet Paine's eyes.

"I don't think you will ever be a success as a politician," said Isobel half kindly. "You're too self-conscious."

"It's extremely unlikely I shall get the chance to try now."

"I mind much more about Robert," said Isobel. "What a fool I've been."

"You might think of something more original to say."

"All right. Listen to this." She leaned forward. "I've remembered about Minny's clothes."

Christopher looked at her a little uncertainly over the top of the glass: he had got his whisky. "Really?"

"Oh, you're too drunk to take in the importance of

what I'm telling you." Isobel stood up, grasped her dark crocodile handbag (from Paris) and straightened her Mirman hat. The two thousand had at least paid for that. She beckoned to Poppet Paine who at once got up and came trotting over. "Here Poppet, you take over. End of act three, scene three."

"Actress," said Christopher just a little more unsteadily than before.

"He's really not too bad, Poppet, keep him off the bottle and out of the police courts and you ought to have quite a life together."

"I've said for a long time that she was a fundamentally vulgar person," said Poppet, justifiably angry.

"She's upset," said Christopher. He added incoherently "Money."

"Well, thank heaven, owing to Daddy I have no need to worry over that. Christopher, let me get a taxi."

Isobel walked out of the restaurant and down the Strand; she had no clear idea where she was walking but her expensive crocodile shoes seemed to know their own mind and turned her in the direction of Pontifex Passage and home. It had been raining, although it had now stopped and the pavements were covered with a thick greasy mud. Isobel tramped on through mud and puddles. The elegance of her appearance, donned for this last meeting with Christopher, was gradually splashed with mud, the grey velvet suit with the fur collar began to look pockmarked and her high-heeled shoes to sag at the back. She took no notice of the fast-moving traffic and several times she only just drew back in time before a taxi or a bus, and these backward jumps into dirty gutters did not improve her looks. She had pushed at her hat so that the curve of fur to match her suit had got misplaced and sat at a queer angle on her head; her hair, which she was wearing long these days, had got dishevelled with the speed of her walk and looked bedraggled. But Isobel was sunk in her own world so that she did not notice, or perhaps no longer cared, how she looked.

At one of her jumps to avoid a passing car she had slightly twisted her ankle and at the same time she dropped a glove; with a last effort to retrieve appearances she popped the remaining glove in her handbag, and so gloveless and limping she went on her way.

At intervals she giggled to herself.

When she got to her own front door in Pontifex Passage it was late afternoon (she had several times lost her way on the journey), and she was unable to find her key.

Karen who answered the door was shocked at her face and made her go straight upstairs to bed. None of her family was at home. Robert was out. Perdita was with Tom, and the children were with their grandmother. Only Karen and Mrs. Daft were in the kitchen together when Isobel came home.

Mrs. Daft crept up the stairs and peeped into the bedroom.

Isobel was lying in bed, she had swallowed a number of sleeping tablets but they had not worked yet and she was laughing and weeping at the same time.

Mrs. Daft came forward and sniffed. "Not drunk," she said.

"Certainly not."

"Loopy," said Mrs. Daft to herself. Aloud she said, "Have a nice cup of tea, dear?"

"It's so awfully funny, Mrs. Daft," said Isobel in gasps, "to have been in love with somebody and then suddenly not to love them any more."

"I'm glad you think so, dear," said Mrs. Daft. "I get more of a laugh out of Danny Kaye myself."

"And the other thing is I've remembered what happened about Minny's clothes, the ones that were hanging up in poor old Mr. Booth's cupboard. I've remembered what really happened to them. I gave them away. Don't you remember?"

"You are in a state, dear," said Mrs. Daft with sympathy. "I should forget it all and have a nice rest."

"Forget it? I've only just remembered."

"Well, I say forget it," said Mrs. Daft firmly, "and have a nice cup of tea if you can't rest. In my opinion, dear, you don't know what you do forget and what you remember. You aren't yourself by a long way."

"Good," said Isobel. "A much better thing not to be myself. A much, much better thing," she added dreamily.

Mrs. Daft tucked Isobel in very firmly, arranged a heap of pillows behind her head and plugged in, over her mistress's faint protests, the electric blanket.

She then departed, giving a longing look at the key in the door as she went. In her belief Isobel would be better locked in. "Well, you're safe there for a bit," she said to herself. "You don't look inclined to get up and make mischief, I will say that for you. Good job I've had practice in dealing with people like old Mr. Booth."

"Is that you talking aloud or me?" asked Isobel idly. She was beginning to feel the effect of the nembutal.

"You," said Mrs. Daft shortly and departed.

Once down in the kitchen Mrs. Daft put her hat and coat on and picked up her big black bag. "Take her up some tea, Karen, like a good girl. I'll have another cup while you're gone."

"Was that the telephone?" said Karen on her return. She had been gone some time.

"I didn't hear it. Don't you start imagining things."

"I don't imagine things. Not me. I am the only sane person in this house."

"You ought to get a doctor to my lady upstairs."

"A doctor? We have had enough of doctors in this house. What can a doctor do for her?"

"I don't know. Soothe her down. Nerves."

"Nerves, that is a good word for it."

"Is she," Mrs. Daft hinted delicately, "like this often?"

"We see here," said Karen cryptically.

"No doubt you do, my dear," said Mrs. Daft into her teacup, "but if you do see, why don't you say what you see? Foreigners are all alike for hinting. I dare say you don't know as much about it as you'd like me to think. Well, I know you don't." She put down her cup. "I shall go now while the police aren't about. Getting proper fed up I am at having them always follow me."

"They have not followed me."

"Well, you never go anywhere do you dear? I'm off, Karen, thanks for the tea."

She scuttled out of the kitchen door and up the area steps. There was no one to be seen. All the debris connected with the death of the constable had been cleared away and only a solitary policeman remained to keep out sightseers. Pontifex Passage was peaceful and quiet.

The constable knew Mrs. Daft and saluted her.

"Just off, Mum?"

"No, I've got to pop into Mr. Cobley's and see to his supper. 'Just leave out something cold,' he said. A nice quiet gentleman. Oh, well, it's a nice peaceful night after a bad day. I wonder you don't feel nervous standing here just where that other poor lad was killed, although, of course, you're in uniform and he wasn't."

"Oh, no, I'm not nervous," said the young man valiantly. "But there is one thing . . . Mrs. Daft, have the little girls gone away?"

"All except Miss Perdita. They've gone to their granny's. Not that they're allowed to call her granny. I'd have let my little granddaughter call me gran if she'd lived, the little love."

"Yes," said the constable. He was not really listening to the indignant old lady. "But you know I think I saw one of the little girls at the end of the road just now. Just for a moment, in the dusk, I couldn't be sure but I think it was."

Perdita had spent the day with Fanny. They had been the last of all to hear the news of the death of the constable. After Perdita's storm of tears of the day before she had slept heavily. Fanny had not slept well, but she had put on her pretty frilly nightgown and stretched herself on her bed and buried her face in the pillow and tried to pretend that when morning came it would be a good day and a happy day. Naturally after this she got up with a bad headache and a prickly feeling of irritation. Two strong cups of coffee and several aspirins removed her headache, but did not begin to touch her temper; in addition the aspirin had made her very gloomy; aspirins always affected Fanny this way.

Perdita, of course, having worked her mood off the day before, rose briskly and cheerfully. This did not improve the day for Fanny.

"Do keep still for a moment, Perdita," she asked.

"Oh, but I feel so much better today."

"But I don't. Keep quiet and crawl round, can't you?"

"It's going to be a good day," said Perdita optimistically.

But the arrival of their employer with a sober look on his face and a newspaper under his arm made them realise how wrong Perdita was.

"I see I'm the bearer of the news again," he said, after looking at their innocent faces.

"What do you mean?" asked Fanny snatching the paper.

"Oh, you won't find it *there*. Be in the midday papers perhaps. If the police release it."

"Is it mother?" asked Perdita grasping his arm.

"Don't be silly," said Fanny, but her face was very white. "Come on, Poldy, don't be a ghoul. Tell us."

Nothing loth, for he loved to have a story to tell, Poldy told them about the death of the constable. He added a few elaborations of his own. "Terribly beaten about, they say. And his clothes all muddy and rained on. Fancy being rained on when you are dead."

"It must happen in lots of wars," said Fanny trembling."

"He was so nice," said Perdita. "I knew him."

"I shouldn't talk too much about that," said Poldy significantly.

"Oh, I'm all right," said Perdita, not pretending not to understand him. "I've got an alibi. I was right here with Fanny."

"Yes, so you were," agreed Fanny thoughtfully.

"Lucky you." Poldy was perhaps a little disappointed. It would have given his business enormous cachet to have had one of his employees suspected of murder, and really his business was just a little bit rocky at the moment.

"I'm afraid I'll have to leave your wages this week girls," he said regretfully. "Just till Monday or so. You don't mind?"

"Don't I, though," said Fanny. "What do you think I live on? Air?"

"Well, perhaps Perdita could cash a cheque for me? I'm sure you could buy me up what with your rich grandmother and everything. No need to shake your head like this. You might do it for me when I'm so worried about these murders on top of everything else."

"You don't have to worry," Fanny pointed out. "You didn't know either of them."

"I can worry about my friends, can't I? And you're wrong actually. I knew them both. I thought Constable Evelyn was a particularly nice boy and you can't deny I took Jack's passport photographs."

"Yes, and he didn't like it."

"We weren't actually bosom friends," admitted Poldy, "still deep down underneath we liked each other. Not enough to quarrel with each other, of course."

"Curious ideas you have about affection," said Perdita.

"Oh, you're so paralysingly English, Perdita. Really I should be surprised if men ever find you attractive."

"If I ever murder anyone," said Perdita eyeing him, "it will probably be you. But surprising as it may seem to you I did not murder either Jack or this poor young policeman."

"Nor me," said Fanny.

"Oh, it doesn't surprise me about you, Fanny, I would never expect you to do anything as *active* as killing anyone."

Fanny's little dog crawled off his mistress's lap, where she was brushing and stroking his soft fur, and trotted over to Poldy.

"He likes me," said Poldy. "Dogs can always tell a real friend." He bent down to pat the little creature. Oh, oh, Fanny, take him off my leg, he's pierced the skin." He pulled up his mauve tweed to examine his ankle. "There's a run in my nylons anyway," he said moodily, "my best ones too that *just* match this suit."

"He knows his real friends, you see."

"Well, I shall go." Poldy gathered up his belongings. "I just come round to be helpful and all you've done is be brutal."

There was a ring at the door.

"That'll be the police," said Poldy with interest; he sat down again.

But it was Tom and Berry and not the police. They had, however, seen the police themselves and had been rather shaken by the process.

"They came round before we were up this morning,

before old Daft appeared to do that greasy little bit of cooking she calls our breakfast, and I must say that they were extremely unpleasant in a quiet way. I doubt if they could have been nastier if we'd assassinated the head of the C.I.D. Quite changed from what they were before. There's no doubt about it, killing a policeman is the quickest way to the rope. Even that man Coffin, who I did think had a human soul . . ."

"Photogenic too," observed Poldy. "It's those lovely high cheekbones."

"In short," said Tom, "we are in a bad way. Can you give us breakfast, Fanny? We couldn't seem to fancy Mrs. Daft's burnt offering." He looked anxiously at Perdita as he spoke.

"Better let me do it," said Berry. He was stammering worse than ever this morning. "Fanny can't cook."

"You," said Poldy in scorn. "Look at the way your hand is shaking. You stay here with the two girls. I'll cook breakfast." The dog got up too. "Oh, so you like me now that I'm going to cook, do you, you little devil? Come on then." In a good humour the two went off to the kitchen; Poldy thoughtfully left the door open so that he could hear all that was going on.

"Speak up," he called. "I can't hear what you're saying."

This was not remarkable for Tom and Perdita were muttering to each other on the sofa by the window and Berry and Fanny were sitting silently holding hands.

"I suppose there's one thing," said Tom. "We can all in a way protect each other. I mean we were together in pairs, we can witness that."

"There are g-gaps you know," said Berry, still

stammering. "We didn't sit up all night watching each other. I don't believe it would count. After all you could have gone out, Tom. I sleep soundly, I wouldn't have known. What about you, girls?"

Perdita curled her feet up on the sofa. "I was dead to the world," she said. "But dead."

Fanny said nothing, only looked worried. "There's no reason really why they should suspect us, is there?" she said at last. "We had no reason to kill the policeman."

"Be your age, Fanny," called Poldy over the spluttering bacon of his frying bacon. "It's because of the first murder he was killed."

"I hadn't any reason to kill Jack either," said Fanny faintly.

"Hadn't you?"

Berry got up and stood frowning.

"No, sit down," said Fanny even more faintly.

"Yes, do," said Poldy as he came in with the bacon and a large pot of coffee. "I didn't mean anything."

"Sit down, boy," said Tom coming over and putting his hand on Berry's shoulder.

It was right to be worried over Berry these days. He was jerky and irritable and untidy. This was understandable in view of what had been going on but all the same was it not excessive? Tom asked himself.

They sat over the bacon and coffee and although Poldy was a very good cook and the bacon was crisp and the coffee hot and strong (comparing favourably with Mrs. Daft's soggy bacon and watery coffee) there was little conversation, only a broody silence.

"We might as well face it," said Tom suddenly. "We are all frightened. We're frightened that one of us is a murderer, and in addition Perdita is frightened it might be her mother."

"I don't know what I'm frightened of," said Perdita. She pushed her hair back from her face and leaned forward on her elbows. "But I know I'm frightened." She shivered. "But am I frightened of what's outside or what's inside me?"

"Dear little love," said Tom putting his arm round her.

"Well, it'll be almost worth it if it's inspired you to say that," said Perdita, cheering up a little, although there were tears in her eyes. Tom silently handed her a handkerchief. "You might watch out though, suppose I turned into a sort of Lucia di Lammermoor and did you in on our wedding night?"

"The whole point about her is that she didn't want to get married, and you, I take it, do?"

"Dying to," said Perdita with a smile.

"Then let's assume that the murderer is not one of us four here, and I count you out too, Poldy." Poldy bowed. "And go on from there."

"Where to?"

"There's Robert for one."

"I don't want it to be Robert," said Perdita dolefully. "I like him so much and he's been so decent to me. You only see him when he is being stiff and formal, but that's because he's shy, he's the nicest person really."

"There's more in Robert than meets the eye," said Tom. "There must be. He once emptied a plate of bortsch down the drain because he didn't like the flavour. A man who could do that could do a lot."

"What did your mother do?" asked Fanny who found the story fascinating.

"She poured out another plate."

"Don't blame her."

"It was horrible soup," said Perdita, "I remember it well. I don't blame Robert." She looked defiant.

"We might try to find out more about Jack," said Tom. "If it wasn't one of us here, then the murderer must be found among some of the other people he knew. And I suggest the hospital."

"Yes, his real life was there after all," said Fanny and there was hope in her voice. "I always knew that even when I didn't want it to be true. Oh, you might as well know, Berry, that not so long ago, just when I started to get to know you, I loved Jack terribly, in a hateful horrible sort of way, because you see he didn't love me. I didn't want you to know."

"Bless you, my girl, I know that. Everyone who knows you knows that." Berry sounded more confident and amused than he had done for some time.

"Even me," said Poldy, who was finishing his plate of bacon. "And as a matter of fact, my dear souls, owing to my friendship with the Press I know one or two things that you don't," and eating the last bite of his bacon, he told them all about Jack's early life in France with his sister, and even, for he was surprisingly well informed, told them about the remark of Jack's that he 'really had a mad one on his hands'! He did not know about Jack and Isobel gambling with the franc but he did say that everyone strongly believed that Jack was 'up to something'.

"Oh, well, poor thing," said the ever sympathetic Perdita.

"I wish we knew what," said Tom.

"It might explain everything," said Fanny. "I think we ought to go to the hospital and go now."

So they set off together in Berry's little car. Poldy bade them farewell on the pavement.

"Dearly should I love to come," he said, "but I am engaged to photograph the features of a rising young television starlet who thinks that I will produce a glamorous portrait and do it more cheaply than one of the big names."

"She little knows," said Fanny.

"I shall get my price," said Poldy modestly.

"Remember to get it in cash, then you can pay your two employees."

The little car jerked forward so suddenly that Poldy's parting words were almost lost.

"Ask for Sister Antrobus," he called out.

Fanny leaned back in the car and relaxed. "I've no doubt he's right," she said. "But how did he know?"

"Poldy knows too much I reckon," said Berry. He had not quite forgiven Poldy for his remark to Fanny. She patted his hand and tucked it with her own inside the big muff of red fox that she was carrying. "Something is licking me," complained Berry, rapidly withdrawing his hand.

"Only my darling little dog," said Fanny, "he's just inside my muff."

"I won't share your affections with a dog," said Berry, raising an amused eyebrow.

"Oh, not share, darling, rather contend for."

Berry's car stopped, as if it were a well trained horse, outside the Victory public house.

"Supposing we all go in," he suggested, "and have a drink before we go on to the hospital."

"Too early," said Fanny.

"Lovely," said Tom.

The barmaid, who was the only occupant of the room, was not too well pleased to see the return of Fanny and her dog. She had clear memories of their last visit. But she conscientiously assumed her professional air of cheerfulness.

"Nice day," she said.

"Brandies," said Tom with a quick look at his party; except for Fanny, who retained her elegance under any conditions, they were a ramshackle and depressed-looking group.

The barmaid was nervous too. "Bad luck about that poor young constable wasn't it?" she said shakily. "Oh, I knew he was asking for it."

"What can you mean?"

"Going round asking questions. He asked the wrong one I reckon."

"But that's what the police are for," said Fanny, putting her arms on the bar and speaking very slowly. For some reason she had constituted herself the vindicator of the dead constable. "They are supposed to ask questions and find out things."

"I heard him in here myself one night," said the woman, ignoring Fanny, "when a customer says to him: 'Who did this murder in Pontifex Passage? I bet the police haven't a clue.' 'Oh, they know, mum,' he answers in a quiet voice. 'They gets there by asking one or two little questions, such as where were *you* when he was murdered?' and he smiles, but I thinks to myself, ask *that* question on a dark night to the wrong person and you'll be for it. And I was right, wasn't I?"

"He did his job," said Fanny, resting herself against the bar. "And now you do yours. Where's the brandy?"

The barmaid slapped their drinks down before them and, having been once rebuffed, tried to talk no more. They drank quickly and departed.

"Don't forget your dog, miss," she called out after them.

At the hospital they hesitated in the huge crowded entrance hall and looked around with nervous faces.

"Hospitals always g-give me a headache," said Berry, beginning to stammer again.

Fanny was looking round her with wide eyes. "You know there's something awfully attractive about a nurse's uniform."

"And you know now what it attracts," said Perdita, who had also been looking round.

Everywhere nurses were hurrying, some carrying great piles of equipment, others pushing patients in chairs, a few carrying nothing but still almost running.

"Yes, hard work," said Fanny regretfully. "They've all got lovely complexions too."

"Haven't you been inside a hospital before?"

"Well, frankly no, darling. That is I believe I was born inside one but naturally I don't remember that, and I have to admit I've kept away from them as being madly unglam. I was wrong though." Her eye was resting on a tall and extremely elegant man who was studying a type-written paper in an aloof way. "Shall I ask him where Sister Antrobus is? He looks as though he knew his way about here."

She advanced carrying the muff and the dog and her

new long antelope handbag (a present from the baron). "Please," she said, parting her lips in her most photogenic smile, "I can see you know absolutely everything there is to know about this hospital, please can you tell me where to find Sister Mary Antrobus?"

Fanny's appearance worked its usual magic and the man regarded her with a more pleased and helpful expression than was perhaps customary with him.

"Sister Antrobus? I don't know, what does she look like?"

"Don't you know?"

"Unfortunately not, although if it would help you, dear lady"—Fanny increased the width of her smile—"I wish I did." He led the way across the floor.

"Oh, thank you," said Fanny tripping beside him; she dropped her muff and as he stooped to pick it up she obligingly let him carry it and the dog. They were both moulting, so she was glad to be rid of them for a bit.

At a long counter in the corner stood a group of women in white coats. They were filling in forms and consulting card indexes.

"I wonder if they can help," said Fanny, and went over to them, still accompanied by her escort. He was having trouble with the dog, though, and had rather dropped behind.

"Can I see Sister Antrobus?" Fanny asked. "Can I see Sister Antrobus?" she asked a few minutes later, but still politely. "Can I see Sister Antrobus?" she shouted.

"You need a red card, patient," said one of the women kindly but absently.

"Well, give me a red card then," said Fanny. She took the red card and looked about for the dog, her muff and her escort. He was struggling, red in the face now, with the peke. "*You* take the red card," said Fanny tucking it in his hand. He dropped it at once. "Not very bright, poor thing," said Fanny to herself.

She was stopped and her shoulder tightly gripped by a tall nurse with an air of authority. "Patient, patient, what are you doing? Mr. Fraser is a *consultant*."

"Really?" said Fanny. "Well, I certainly wouldn't have made him carry things if I'd known that, but he looks perfectly healthy." She caught sight of the nurse's face. "Are you sure you are feeling well?" she asked kindly. "It's nothing catching is it?" She took her muff and her dog and the red card from Mr. Fraser and gave him another charming smile. "I do hope you will be better soon."

To the nurse she said: "All I want is Sister Antrobus."

"I *am* Sister Antrobus."

Fanny turned the full power of her personality on Sister Antrobus. "Now, let's be perfectly frank with each other," she said, "my friends and I," and she beckoned to the other three who were standing in a group for protection, "must see Sister Antrobus."

"I've told you. I am Sister Antrobus."

"Then we want to talk to you about Jack. You know who I mean?"

"There's nothing I can tell you about him that you don't know." The fierceness faded and Sister Antrobus looked tired. "You're Fanny, I suppose."

"Yes," said Fanny, puzzled and flattered. "How do you know?"

Sister Antrobus smiled. "There can't be more than one like you. Debonair and gay and very lovely."

"Did Jack say that? I'm touched."

"He also added—and a chattering little idiot."

"Oh. Not quite fair."

The group assembled round Sister Antrobus. She looked into their hopeful eyes and shook her head.

"Yes, I can see why you are worried. But I can't tell you anything you don't know."

"So we are at a dead end," said Fanny.

"We were silly to expect anything," said Perdita.

"I suppose it's your little sister that Jack was so worried about? He wanted to protect the child. I wonder if he succeeded? Is she safe and well?"

"I hope so," said Perdita.

"You hope so? You're pretty casual aren't you? All eaten up by your own concerns. Has any one of you taken the trouble to see if the child is safe?"

She turned her back on them in scornful dismissal. "Well, good-bye. Give my respects to your father, Miss Duveen. I saw him in court once."

"I can see you know a lot of people from Pontifex Passage."

"I also know Mrs. Daft. And Mr. Booth of course," She frowned. "He's probably going home today."

"You could fill a ward with us, couldn't you?" asked Perdita with misplaced brightness.

"Yes, the psychiatric," she said and turned on her heel.

"She wasn't very nice to us," said Perdita.

"She's under pressure," answered Tom, "and very unhappy."

"It was you and me she didn't like chiefly," said Fanny looking at the rigid and retreating back.

"And can't you see why?" Tom asked. "She was in love with Jack. Oh, well, she'll get over it I suppose. He's dead. She'll forget."

"Yes," said Perdita, "and that's the saddest thing of all isn't it? The poor dead, dull and forgotten." She put her hand in Tom's. "Perhaps I have been slack about Minny. I'd like to go home now."

They were slow getting home. The little car needed attention at a garage and in the end they had to walk home to Pontifex Passage. Perdita was getting more and more uneasy

She let herself in at the front door of her home.

Karen met her and in an anguished voice told her that not long ago from an upstairs window she had seen Minny walk down Pontifex Passage; she had rushed out to meet her but by the time she had got to the door the child was gone. Karen burst into tears.

"Life is what you make it," said Coffin unhappily as he and the superintendent trudged once more round to Pontifex Passage, this time to call on the difficult and elusive Mr. Cobley.

"And death is what you don't." This near approach to an epigram brought Coffin round to stare at the superintendent with surprise:

"You could put it that way I suppose. Look at this boy, Evelyn, he joins the police, does well, works for promotion, then because he has the bad luck to come across a murderer he's dead before his time. But then he had chosen to go into the Force and take that sort of risk, and that's what I meant by life being what you make it."

"And he died because he didn't make a due report to his superior at the proper time and so ran unnecessary risks that no one asked him to make. We could have saved him. And that's what *I* meant."

His subordinate sighed. "I hope the worst thing that could happen has happened. I feel uneasy."

They rang the bell of Mr. Cobley's house and after a long pause they saw Mrs. Daft poke her face round the door.

"Is Mr. Cobley at home?"

"Well, he is and he isn't."

"By which you mean?"

"He's been in and gone out again. There's no one here but me. I'm getting him a bit of cold supper."

Certainly Mrs. Daft herself had been eating for there were crumbs and traces of chocolate round her mouth. She smiled at the policemen.

"However, I don't suppose he'll be back to eat it."

"No?"

"He came dashing in just now to say that he was getting married the day after next, and then he went off again. It isn't likely that a gentleman who is getting married the day after next and then going abroad will come back and eat a cold supper is it?"

"No, I suppose not. Going abroad you say?"

"Bound to be, I know the signs. So I'm the only one at home." The door was closing again.

"We did want to see Mr. Cobley."

"It doesn't look as though you will."

"He'll be back some time."

"Will he?" Mrs. Daft was shaking with laughter, or Coffin supposed it was with laughter, she was screwing her face up as if in mirth. Through the door he could see a little of the house. It was decorated with an air of richness, with thick carpets (none the better perhaps for being looked after by Mrs. Daft) and heavy silk curtains. Coffin thought that there was one thing all the inhabitants of Pontifex Passage had in common, and that was an impulse towards a high standard of living.

"Suppose we come in and wait?"

"And suppose you don't."

The sergeant grinned. "Well, as we didn't come here for a tête-à-tête with you perhaps you're right." And then he wondered what was keeping Winter so quiet.

Winter was examining a small object he had in his hand.

"Found this outside the gate," he said and held it out.

It was a small pink glove.

"That's Minny's," said Mrs. Daft.

At that moment the constable on duty pushed open the gate, came up to Winter and saluted.

"Message just come through for you, sir." He lowered his voice. "The child Minny Duveen is missing from her grandmother's house."

Although he had whispered Mrs. Daft heard him. "They should never have sent her away. She's an affectionate child and she loves her mother. That child's gone to be with her mother."

"I'll be obliged if you'll say nothing more," said Winter, pocketing the glove; he gave the old lady one of his sharper looks.

"The salt of the earth that old woman," said Coffin as they departed.

"I was robbed of fivepence-halfpenny when I was a boy of six by a woman very like that," said Winter austerely.

A slight mist was blowing up from the river and settling over the park where the school children had played. It was thicker over Pontifex Passage.

"Not a nice night for a little girl to be out by herself," said Winter.

"That's the best we can hope for," said Coffin. "That she *is* by herself."

CHAPTER ELEVEN

MINNY DUVEEN WAS not with her mother, although Isobel was awake and up in spite of all her sleeping tablets. A telephone call made by her to Lady Passey to find out how the girls were had brought only the bewildering and terrifying reply, "But I put her in the bus and sent her home just as you telephoned and asked!"

"No one telephoned and no one asked," said Isobel, putting down the telephone. She knew now that she would have to face Robert and Perdita and the police with the news.

Superintendent Winter sent out an all stations alert about Minny, drafted a few short sentences to go on the B.B.C. news, and then sat down to wait.

"Nothing we can do now except wait," he said. "It's getting foggy isn't it?" He went to the window and looked out. "Yes. Early for this time of the year."

The sergeant muttered something under his breath. All that could be heard was the word 'muddle'.

"You may be in one," said Winter, "but I'm not. I know who the murderer is and so ought you by now. You might go and get the constable who was on duty today in Pontifex Passage. He ought to be coming off duty about now."

At the Pontifex Passage Divisional Station the constable was found sitting in the canteen. He was resting and eating a boiled egg. He gave Coffin a startled look when he recognised him, and stood up. He was quite pleased to see the sergeant who was a popular and respected figure.

"Don't get up, dear," said Coffin, squeezing himself into the seat next to the constable. "I've put on weight since I used to eat here. The super wants to see you. But let's both have a cup of tea first. Runs you off your feet, don't it, this case? I suppose you knew Evelyn?"

"We joined the Force together. He was a bit older than me though."

Coffin looked almost affectionately at the smooth round young cheek. "Couldn't very well be much younger," he thought.

"Ambitious, I suppose?"

"Oh, he was. Night school and everything when he could fit it in. He was clever."

"Yes, I'm afraid he was," sighed Coffin.

"I think he'd got at the truth about Dr. O'Finney's death and he knew where the trouble about the little girl started from. He knew the people you see, and that counts. Superintendent Winter comes down here for the first time when the murder is done. He can't tell which of all the people concerned is the sort to do murder."

There was no impertinence intended in this innocent criticism and Coffin found none.

"He's had a lot of experience though," he pointed out. "We'd better get off I think. He's not down at the D.O. today, he sent me in the car to pick you up."

Winter took the young man through an account of his whole day on duty. Whom had he seen, whom had he talked to, what had he noticed. At the end he leaned back and studied the notes he had made with a satisfied look, as if he had got what he wanted.

"You are sure you have told me everything? This is the most complete account you can remember? I can trust you on the detail?"

The young man nodded confidently.

"Then you can go now. Thank you."

Winter too stood up and put his coat on. "Out we go again. I shall want you, Coffin, to come too."

The police car drove them through what was now a light mist rather than fog. There was still no news of Minny.

Coffin knew what the chances were. "If we don't find her within the next eight hours then she is dead."

The car stopped outside the door of the Victory; the named was outlined in pale green lights but something was defective and it was flickering irritably.

The barmaid looked up as they came in and sighed.

"You again."

"We want a word with you."

"I was afraid of that."

"Come on, my girl, don't pull such a long face."

"Look, it's no treat to me to have to go over all this again. I'm a nice cheerful sort of girl and I like to talk about nice cheerful things. All this business is making me morbid. Only yesterday my young man said to me, 'Well, Dot, you are a wet week today,' and it's not good enough," she said leaning forward and staring earnestly in Winter's face. "I've got to keep cheerful, it's my job, customers don't want their beer handed to them as if it was a dose of chloroform. A joke's my stock in trade."

"I can see what you mean."

"And then it's particularly important for me to keep lively for my young man on account of his job. He works in the hospital you know, a very good quiet job." She coughed and lowered her voice delicately. "Where they go when they don't quite get better," she said.

"Eh?" Coffin looked blank.

"She means the mortuary," said Winter with impatience.

"That's right. So naturally when it's his time off duty he likes a bit of life and conversation. 'Come on, Dot,' he says, 'show me the difference between work and play.'"

"Well, all right," said Winter, "but all I want——"

"And then you know," said Dot virtuously, "this is such a respectable neighbourhood. No Haighs or Heaths round here."

"Well, you've got a homicidal maniac now," said Winter.

"Oh, Lord." Dot put down the bottle of whisky she was holding. "Are you sure? Oh, how unwholesome."

The superintendent, having thus stunned her in lieu of an anaesthetic, extracted her information like an old lightly rooted tooth. She told him again about Jack O'Finney and the young policeman in detail, using the same words she had used to him before, and to the young people from Pontifex Passage.

"But I've told you all this before," she said with the anxiety of someone who feels the dentist has taken the wrong tooth out.

"You'll swear to its complete accuracy?"

"Course I do," she said apprehensively. "But I

won't have to will I? I wouldn't like to appear in court."

"You'd get your expenses."

"I wasn't thinking of the money," said the unhappy girl.

"Come on," said Winter who had a sharp eye. "You haven't told us everything."

"Or we haven't asked the right question," said Coffin.

"Ask it then."

But there was no need. "I believe I know who did these murders," said Dot miserably. "The constable told me. He didn't give no name but I could guess from the description. And he must have been right, mustn't he?" she said simply. "Because he died."

"What did he say to you?"

"He said: 'You mustn't judge her too hardly. She's not had much of a life, poor thing. Her husband died insane and that daughter of hers is unstable. It's not surprising if her mind is touched.' Well, I knew what he meant. I worked for Lady Passey when I was a girl, we all knew about poor Miss Isobel's first husband. The family belong to this district like I do, Miss Isobel's husband died in the hospital round the corner and all her children were born there, including that Perdita (and she does act funny sometimes). I was glad when she married Mr. Duveen, he's ever so nice, but it doesn't look as if she was meant to be happy does it?" The girl was in tears.

All roads seemed to lead to Isobel Duveen.

The Hospital of St. Clare, to which the two policemen inevitably went next, received them but it could not be said to welcome them.

Coffin was unhappy. "I wish there was news of the child."

"This is the quickest way of finding her."

"Well, what do you want now?" asked the Administrator, Mr. Spring, wearily.

"I want to be allowed to examine some case histories."

"They wouldn't mean much to you. Only to a doctor or a nurse."

"Then give me a doctor or a nurse too."

Mr. Spring rang two bells. Red lights flashed in a panel over his door.

"I wish I knew what you wanted," he said.

"I expect to find what I want," said Winter heavily, "among the records of births and deaths."

CHAPTER TWELVE

KAREN, WHO HAD worked for so long in the background of the Duveens' lives now suddenly pushed herself into the front. Or, more accurately, she was pushed.

"I blame myself terribly," said Fanny. "But how could I tell? He's never bitten anyone before."

"Had some good tries," said Tom, looking at the peke. "Karen wasn't quick enough."

"I expect she'd have given notice anyway," said Perdita. "She was heading for a blow-up. I don't blame you. Or her for that matter."

Karen had leaned forward to talk to Fanny, in a none too pleasant way perhaps, but still meaning to be friendly enough, and she had peered into Fanny's face in her short-sighted way only to have the dog pop its head smartly out of the muff and nip her nose.

She had no need, everyone agreed, of the bandages, brandy and anti-rabies shots that she so loudly demanded.

"Teeny weeny little scratch," said Fanny soothingly. "You can hardly see it."

"Dog's not mad," said Berry.

"Anyway, he's very little," said Perdita.

"His teeth are big enough," said Karen.

"I always thought she spoke English better than she admitted," said Perdita afterwards, "and the way she carried on then proved it. But she had no need to talk about damages."

"I honestly don't think it was that," said Tom thoughtfully. "She was just getting over that. We were calming her down. It was what happened afterwards."

"So far as I am concerned," Perdita said firmly, "nothing happened."

"You'll have a job maintaining that attitude if she does make a case out of it."

"*I* certainly did not see anything hit her on the head."

"Naturally not, you had your head in Fanny's muff, but you must have heard."

After the dog-bite they had all stood in the hall reassuring Karen and urging her to tell all that she knew about Minny. There was a certain amount of restless movement about because, as Perdita said, they were upset. Berry had perched the little dog on top of an antique tallboy in walnut that Isobel kept in the square dark hall. There was nothing on the top of the tallboy except the dog and the little creature was too sensible to jump so one might have supposed he was safe.

Unluckily, however, Isobel had chosen to hang up on the wall next to the tallboy the large bearskin that her grandfather had shot while out on a visit in 1896 to the Romanovs. Isobel had hung it head upmost so that its eyes were on a level with the dog. Naturally, as soon as he saw it, the brave little dog, remembering that Fanny had often said that his breed were called 'Little Lion' in China, flung himself upon this large furry head. Perhaps having tasted Karen his success had gone to his head.

He launched himself upon the bear's head, and though he made very little impression on the tough and aged animal he dislodged the screws which were keeping the bear upright on the wall. There was a tearing sound, a cloud of dust, and the bear fell forward.

Of course it fell upon Karen and the jaws fastened themselves neatly around her throat. She screamed loudly.

Perdita, who had had a good deal to bear lately, buried her hysterical giggles in Fanny's muff so that she missed the moment when Tom rushing forward to free Karen knocked over the telephone which struck Karen on the head.

Karen's version of the events was that she had been bitten and attacked both by Perdita and her friends. Although not strictly true there was a lot of truth in it.

"You are dreadful people," she said standing stiffly with the bearskin round her ankles and gripping the telephone with both hands. The dog was barking wildly in the background, much pleased presumably by his success in downing the large furry creature who, he could now see quite clearly, was dead.

"Oh, shut up," said Tom trying to give him a quietening blow.

The front door opened to admit Robert and at the same time the telephone rang in Karen's hands. She dropped it with a scream.

"What is this pandemonium?" asked Robert; he stooped to pick up the telephone.

Berry and Fanny looked embarrassed and moved towards the door. "We'd better go perhaps," said Fanny.

"It might be a good idea," observed Robert coldly.

"Sir," said Tom.

"Well?" Robert was not yet used to the idea of young men calling him sir. These young Guards officers, he thought.

"Better push off, Tom," said Perdita bitterly. "This is strictly family."

Robert looked at her apprehensively and bent towards the telephone which had now stopped ringing. "What is all this?" he asked.

Several miles away Lady Passey put the receiver back on her telephone and sank back into the feeling of helplessness which she was getting used to now in dealing with her daughter's affairs.

"They're all mad at Pontifex Passage," she said with horrid and unconscious aptness. "First they ring up and say send Minny round and then when I try to ring them again there's no answer." She paused. "I suppose it *was* a message from Isobel the first time. Oh, but I knew the voice. I can trust *her*."

She sat down in her charming drawing-room. The house had belonged to her present husband's first wife, and although Lady Passey had re-done the house completely from top to bottom, disinfected it practically, so that had the ghost of the former lady returned she would certainly not have known her way about, it had not been possible to do anything about the ceiling which was decorated with hearts and her predecessor's initials intertwined with those of Sir Lane Passey. It angered Lady Passey to have to endure this but her architect had advised her that to touch it would endanger the structure of the whole room.

Sir Lane shuffled into the room. He was not very old but idleness had brought him soon to infirmity, and although he could still, when necessary, escort his wife to a night-club, at home he often went in slippered ease. He was particularly tired at the moment as he had been playing poker with the twins.

"Card-sharpers you know," he said. "Real little card-sharpers. Got a look of you, Char'."

"I don't know about that," said his wife. "Lane, give me what is left of your mind for a bit. I'm worried."

"Well, we all are, aren't we?" said Sir Lane simply. "One damn' thing after another, isn't it?"

"I should never have let Minny go off even although it was what her mother asked."

"No, that's what I thought."

"Why on earth didn't you say so?"

"You never listen to me Char' old girl. I remember the time when I said to you, Char' don't wear that black hat today and you said, 'Shut up, you know nothing about it.' And that wasn't the only time. I remember once in Capri . . ."

"But those were unimportant things," wailed Lady Passey. "Of course I didn't listen, there's no comparison."

"As you never listened to me about unimportant things it never struck me you'd listen to me about important things," said Sir Lane simply.

"I always listen to you about my investments," said his wife in tears.

"Yes, money is my job," said Sir Lane gravely, "and the children are yours and Isobel's, and a precious poor job you seem to have made of it each in your turn."

The twins came into the room in search of company. "You ran away because we were winning," they said accusingly.

"Quite right."

"Please go back upstairs, twins," said their grandmother. "I'm worried."

"You know it was silly of you to let Minny go off like that." They looked serious.

"So I'm beginning to think."

"You have to watch over Minny. You can't be quite sure about what she says."

"Children, do you mean she tells lies?"

"She's only five. You can't call it lies. But she doesn't always say what is true."

The words exploded in Lady Passey's mind. Had the whole worry about Minny been based then on a deception? If so then there had there never been a man? The murders were real enough though.

"Supposing," she thought, "all the time we were watching over Minny we should really have been watching someone else."

Then the telephone rang again. And this time it *was* Isobel.

In the kitchen Karen was packing her bags and saying that she would not, could not stay in this house a minute longer.

In the drawing-room Isobel, Robert and Perdita waited for the arrival of Lady Passey.

"Karen says Mrs. Daft won't be coming back," announced Robert.

"Another rat leaving the sinking ship," said Perdita.

"It's not the actual sinking I mind so much," said Robert, "as this dreadful uncertainty, the not knowing whether one's going to be struck by lightning or hit by a torpedo: Act of God or act of the police."

"You'll mind the sinking all right when it actually happens," said Perdita grimly.

"I shouldn't call poor old Mrs. Daft a rat exactly," said Isobel; she seemed not to have taken in that Mrs. Daft was leaving. Her hair was tidy and pushed back from her face, her eyelids were puffy and red, her face almost unmade up; she looked years older but tougher and more resolute.

Lady Passey came puffing into the room. She had remembered to put on her fashionable top coat and her Paris hat, but she had forgotten to take off her velvet house shoes.

"Had to let myself in, where are all your people?" she panted. "I came over at once. I must say, Isobel, you have been madly careless about this child."

"*I* have, Mother? You seem to have dispatched her from your house into the blue with more enthusiasm than foresight."

"Oh, Mother, how can you be *angry*," cried Perdita, "when we don't even know where Minny is? Anger's no *use*."

"Of course I'm angry," said Isobel. "Do you suppose I'm sitting down under so pointless an emotion as misery? I'm angry and I'm going to do something. We are all to blame about Minny and I am most to blame, of course. I see that clearly enough."

Robert got up and assumed his best cross-examining manner. Unconsciously the three women grouped themselves together. He was the accuser and they were the accused.

"Before you start doing anything, Isobel, I'd like to talk to you all." Talking, to Robert, naturally meant asking questions.

He directed himself first to Lady Passey.

"You had a telephone call asking you to send Minny round to us? Man's voice?"

"A woman's of course. That is why I accepted it for what it pretended to be. I'd have been suspicious of a man."

"And why were you so certain it was from Isobel?"

"Well, I was expecting a message from Isobel, of course. It was partly that, I suppose."

"Why?"

Lady Passey shifted uneasily. "Oh, well, she had said she would ring, and then of course that line of yours has a funny echoing quality and I suppose I thought I heard that too. I *did* hear it. That call was made from here."

"I see." Robert looked down at his cuff. "What about you, Perdita? You didn't telephone from here?"

"Oh, no, of course I didn't, how can you think it of me?" Perdita was near tears. "I love poor little Minny. I know I didn't ring. Unless I'm a complete and utter loony which always has to be considered I suppose, I didn't know anything about Minny being missing till I got in and heard that Karen thought she had seen her wandering on her own in Pontifex Passage It wasn't till I heard from mother that she had telephoned Granny that I grasped what had really happened."

195

"Yes, I can see you've been worried, and I think it is about Minny."

"Oh, it is," said Perdita with emphasis. "Just for once I haven't been thinking about me at all."

"And you were worried too?" said Robert turning to his mother-in-law.

"Sick with it," said Lady Passey briefly.

"Yes, you've both acted worried all along. But Isobel," and her husband turned towards her, "hasn't acted worried. Not at all in the way you would expect. That has worried *me*."

His wife gave him a cold stare.

"Isobel hasn't acted worried because I believe she hasn't been worried. Until now you haven't really believed Minny was in any sort of trouble, have you, Isobel?"

Isobel made a movement which could have been either denial or assent.

"And could this have been because you really knew all the time exactly what was going on?"

"No, that's not really true."

But her husband ignored her. "And if so, why are you worried now? Isobel, why are you worried now?"

He took her arm.

"The trouble with you," said Isobel, shaking his hand away, "is that you haven't the faintest idea what you are talking about." She said this not insolently, not angrily, not challengingly, but as if lost in thoughts that Robert could not possibly understand. "No, please don't touch me again. You're a bad judge of character, Robert, I've said so before and I dare say I will again. You haven't understood Minny's character."

"What do you mean?"

"Don't you wonder why I am dressed like this, Robert? I am going out." She turned back at the door. "You've jumped to a lot of conclusions. You assumed that it was my voice Mother thought she heard on the telephone. But she said it was a 'message' from me. Why don't you ask her whose voice she thought she heard?"

Karen, packing in the kitchen, paused in her task. She heard a door bang, feet on the stairs and a door bang again. She could hear voices. She listened for a moment and then went back to her work.

"Mad," she said.

She too, in her way, was a poor judge of character.

CHAPTER THIRTEEN

REPORTS ABOUT MINNY DUVEEN began to come in.

Almost at once a woman telephoned from Worthing to say that she had seen Minny walking along the promenade holding a man's hand. The man was aged fifty.

"Took out his birth certificate, I suppose," grumbled Winter as he discounted it.

An hour later a hefty girl of nine was dragged into Battersea Police Station by a triumphant woman, and in spite of her protests that she was not, would not be, Minny Duveen, and that her name was Letty Broster, she was handed over to a reluctant constable. "An unlikely name," said the woman, "and if you are not the Duveen kid why are you hiding round corners?" "Well, why are you looking round them?" sobbed the child. "Yes, why?" asked the constable with interest. "Seen you before, haven't I?"

Another report came in from Dunoon in Perthshire that Minny had been seen at the opening of the local Bring and Buy Jumble Sale; she had been disguised as a small boy.

"We shall have Sydney, Australia, on the phone next," said Winter. "Do they think this child is rocket propelled?"

More sinister reports from hospitals began to trickle

in. A child like Minny had been run over and was unconscious: a little girl had been brought in at Kensington after a bad fall in a children's playground, no one claimed her, was this Minny? A dead child had been discovered in an old air-raid shelter off the Tottenham Court Road; she was small, dark, well cared for and well dressed. Was this Minny?

Winter got into his car and was silently driven off.

But the child was not Minny.

But soon reports of insignificant yet ominous details began to filter in.

A constable turning in his usual report had noted that a number eleven bus had swerved so rapidly going round the corner at Hyde Park that there had very nearly been an accident. He had taken the number. It so happened that he had seen a little girl wearing a red coat and carrying gloves but not wearing a hat sitting on the seat near the conductor.

Winter took this up. After a little thought he telephoned to the Controller of the South-West London bus depot from which he guessed the bus would have come.

A crisp voice answered him. "Yes, that line ran from this garage." The voice was helpful but cautious. "If the superintendent knew the number and exactly what time the bus turned at Hyde Park Corner it would be possible to identify the bus."

The superintendent did know and he mentally gave the accurate and observant constable a good mark.

There was a long pause with a good deal of chattering in the distance. Winter waited patiently. Coffin walked up and down anxiously. "Stop wasting your time and cneck exactly when the child left her grandmother's," said Winter briefly and turned again to the telephone.

"The bus you want is number thirty-four on the rota," said the voice from the Controller's office. By now Winter found himself irritated by its calm good sense. "I want to speak to the driver and the conductor."

"The driver and his mate will be coming off duty in about three-quarters of an hour."

"I can't wait that long."

There was a shorter pause. "They should be approaching the Hyam Road stop in about twenty minutes. There is always a pause of two minutes there. You could pick them up."

Without hesitation Winter ordered the car. Coffin appeared at the last moment and slipped in beside him. "The times fit," he said quickly. "She could have been the child on the bus. But her granny sent her off in a taxi, and she had no money on her."

He did not know that at that very moment an anxious and frightened taxi-driver was telling Mrs. Duveen how he had started off with Minny from her grandmother's house but that when he had looked round after a long wait in a traffic jam he had seen the taxi empty. "She slipped out, I reckon, and I see her getting on a bus." He admitted that he had been angry and had driven off.

"We can't be sure about the money," said Winter. "The one thing that is clear about this is that Minny Duveen could keep her own secrets." He sighed. "How many men have we on the job of looking for the taxi? Right. We shall pick him up sooner or later. What possessed the child to get out of the taxi?"

"Frightened, I suppose," said Coffin.

"Or someone told her what to do."

The car drew up smoothly beside the Hyam Road stop. A few people were waiting but there was no bus in sight.

"Hope we haven't missed it," said Coffin. He looked at his watch.

"Not if they're on time," said the driver leaning back. "And neither God nor the Depot Controller can be sure of that with traffic the way it is now."

The long black car with two obvious policemen in it did not go unnoticed by the bus queue. There was a certain amount of curious shuffling forward to get a better look.

"Wonder who they're after," said a tall thin man in a grey cap and a check scarf. "They say that Charley boy is on the dodge again."

"Well, I'm glad to say I don't know Mr. Boy or whatever his name is so I couldn't say whether he was dodging or not," said a small plump respectable woman to whom he had addressed himself.

"Ho, well, he is," said the man. "Been on the cars again."

"Cars?"

"Yes, *you* know, car at the kerb, now you see it, now you don't. That's Charley."

"It doesn't sound at all respectable."

"Respectable? No, it's not that. A good trade though. But chancy. That's the police waiting to nick him now, I expect."

"Police is it?" said the woman sniffing. "I thought it was a funeral."

"You would think so, wouldn't you, to see them sitting there so glum but you can't mistake the back of their neck. Police any day. I know."

At that moment a bus drew up and stopped.

Winter approached the conductor and Coffin went round to speak to the driver. Winter's heart sank as he looked at the conductor; he had expected a man and he saw a thick-set stocky woman with grubby hands and a greasy Eton crop. He looked at her gloomily and she looked morosely back. "You'd take the scalp off that one easier than get information out of her," he told himself.

"Full up," she said, passing her hand over the back of her head.

"I'm not getting on."

She studied him. "Well, get off then."

"I'm a police officer. I want some information from you."

"Let's see your cards." She leaned forward.

With a sigh Winter produced them. It was not usual for him to be asked.

"Of course you might have forged them," she said suspiciously.

"Madam, you flatter yourself."

"Well, ask me what you want then. I shan't know the answers of course." She saw the look on his face. "Well, I'm just warning you."

He asked her if she remembered a small girl on the bus earlier that day; a child who might be remembered because she was travelling alone.

She spread her hands out triumphantly. "Told you I wouldn't know."

"It was the run when your bus swerved to avoid another car at Hyde Park Corner."

"Tell me when we don't do that there."

"This child was wearing red," persevered Winter.

"I can't help you," sang out the girl. "Now if you'll get off my bus . . ."

"Now, my girl, you'd better give your mind to this," said Winter exasperated.

"If you want to know where Charley is," said the tall thin man in the cap, lowering his voice to a hoarse whisper. "I could put you on to him for a little of the ready-ready."

"Charley?" said Winter. "Who's talking about Charley?"

"Go on, do you mean to say you're not after him?" said the man disappointed.

"Charley boy," said the police driver. "Inspector Fraser's been after him."

"Ah, I knew someone would be," said the man with relief. "I can tell you where he is. Glad to help."

"You're late, chum. They took him this morning."

"Go on. Poor old Charley."

"Just as well really," said the driver. "If all his friends are like you."

"Well, bye-bye," said the conductress and she banged the bell three times.

"You can't go till I've finished," said Winter.

"Oh, can't I? I go when the driver starts up ".

To his relief Winter saw Coffin coming round the side of the bus with the driver. The bus driver was a large man with an air of good humoured efficiency which he

203

would have to be, no doubt, to drive his Leviathan through the streets of London.

"Now come on, my dear," he said to the conductress. "You can be helpful to these policemen. A nice clever, observant girl like you must have taken a lot in. I know you. Besides it was a nice little kiddy. I know you like kids."

"Can't stand 'em," she said, but she was weakening. She gave the driver a smile and he smiled back and clapped an arm round her shoulder. She was a large girl herself, but she looked frail, although still not feminine, beside her driver. Winter perceived that there was an affection between this tender couple.

"This kid is special, see? We might find later on that she's dead all this time."

"Really?" asked the girl ghoulishly. "She's been done away with? Well, tell me what she was like?"

For answer Winter produced a photograph of Minny; it showed Minny with her sisters and although taken early in the summer it was a good likeness of Minny.

"Yes," said the conductress, tapping her teeth thoughtfully. Winter reckoned that he had seldom seen a girl who had so many unpleasing gestures. "I believe I did see her. But you put me off by saying she was alone."

"Wasn't she?"

"Yes, well she got on alone all right, but someone met her at the stop."

"What was this person like?"

"Oh, I didn't see much." There was a regretful look on her face. "It was a woman though."

"It would be, of course," said Winter. "Where did she get off?"

The girl frowned. "Not sure. Let me think. By Pleasant Park, I think."

Winter nodded.

"I hope I've helped you."

"Yes and no."

The two policemen got back into the car and returned to Winter's office.

Another report had come in while they were away.

A park-keeper had found a pink glove in a rubbish bin in the park near Pontifex Passage. He knew Minny and he knew the glove.

"A bit of intelligence for once," said Winter. "He didn't waste time getting it to us."

In the glove were a bus ticket and a two-shilling piece.

There was something pathetic in the little girl's trick of stowing the ticket and money away in the glove for safety.

"All the same, she lost both gloves," said Winter in a worried way. "I don't like it."

In the minds of both men was the unspoken thought that the hands which should have held these gloves were dead.

"Give it a few more hours," said Coffin. "If we don't get on to her by then we shall have to say she's not alive."

"We'd better go and see this park-keeper."

"He's here," said Coffin. "As you said, he's intelligent. He brought the glove himself."

The park-keeper had changed from his uniform and wore a tweed jacket and grey flannel trousers; but he still looked like a sleepy, benevolent horse. Winter who was no horseman did not find this a thing in his favour, but Coffin who had placed many a bet, thought there must be something to a man who looked as though he might win the Grand National.

"Where did you find this glove?"

"In the rubbish bin," said the man. He added acutely, "And that's a funny thing in itself."

"Yes," said Winter studying him. "In a way it is."

"You see if it was lost by the child, then why was it not just left lying on the path? And if it was put in the bin by some tidy soul, then why was the money left in it?"

"Yes. You've thought it all out I can see. What's your explanation?"

"It's the way a child might get rid of something that it was frightened to keep in its possession," said the man closing his eyes and speaking carefully. "She had the money, you see, say she wasn't supposed to have any money, a child would have to explain that."

"I wish I could explain it," said Winter. "You seem to know a lot about the Duveens."

"Watched them all. Know the whole family. Nice little girls. But they're not ordinary. Something different about them. They get it from their mother. I take an interest."

"I can see you do."

"And I would say that the child's had something on her mind for a long time. She didn't play like the other children in her school, she was quieter, more broody, made up stories to herself. There's something worrying that child, I used to say." He leaned forward to make his point. "And at that age something is more usually *someone* if you see what I mean."

"We know that was true."

"I hear the gossip that is going round. We do in the parks. People stop to pass the time of day with us, talk to us, and without knowing it often hand over odd bits of information. We can piece things together. I know the gossip about Mrs. Duveen. And I know the police have suspected her of the murder and perhaps of having something to do with the trouble over her own child. You're not the only ones, either. But you're wrong."

"Are they all like you that work in the park?" asked Winter, not answering the implied question.

"I'm not going to give you the name of the person I suspect. I see more of life in the park than you think and there's only one person in that set-up that I'd pick as a killer. If you've got any sense you will work it out for yourself."

"If you've got any information you ought to give it to the police."

"What I guess isn't information, but so that you can guess too I'll tell you that the person I'm thinking of has a motive, and from the murderer's point of view a strong motive." He looked at Winter. "You wouldn't know about that of course."

"And supposing I said that I did know? And supposing I said that I agreed with you? And supposing I said that for your own sake you'd better keep your tongue quiet until I've made an arrest?" There was a harsh note in Winter's voice.

"I'll keep my tongue quiet," said the park-keeper. "I haven't been carrying on like this just to impress you. That Minny's a dear little girl. She deserves to be looked after. She's vulnerable, see, because it's her affections that are being played on. That's wicked."

"Yes, that's wicked," agreed Winter gravely.

"All the same, it's funny about the money isn't it?" said Winter as he showed the man out. "If you are right and the child herself placed the money and glove in the bin—then doesn't that seem as if it was her *mother* she was going to see?"

"Yes, I can't explain that," said the keeper with dignity. "I don't know everything, but I tell what I believe to be true. D'ye see?"

Thus they traced the pattern of Minny's movements across the city.

The next piece of information that came in seemed at first to have no connection with Minny and would never have been brought to the superintendent's notice had not the episode turned up in the neighbourhood of Pontifex Passage.

One of the constables making the dull and routine inquiries that Winter had set on foot was asking after Minny in the little sweet shop two turnings away from the passage. It was a crowded shop that gave the impression of selling everything from chocolate mice to coal by the bag. The owner, a stout young man, was interviewed by the constable from behind towering tins of mixed biscuits and packets of detergents. The policeman looked wistfully at the upright chair by the counter, he would have enjoyed taking his considerable weight off his aching feet, but he decided he looked more official and impressive standing up.

The shopkeeper had no information to give. He had

never heard of the Duveens, and as far as he knew had never seen them.

"No," he said chewing a piece of gum, "I've never seen them. Sorry I can't help you," and he watched the policeman walk out.

When he was almost at the door the policeman saw the notice pointing out that coach seats could be booked for long-distance trips here in this shop. "Coaches going everywhere. North, south, east and west," it pointed out.

The policeman's feet ached and he had missed his tea, but he hated being slovenly. (His school reports had said 'Jack is slow but thorough'.) He also remembered the words of one of the lectures he had attended, years ago now, at the Police College. "Take every opportunity, never pass over anything." So reluctantly he turned back.

The shopkeeper took the gum out of his mouth, wrapped it economically in a bit of paper and got out his records.

"I don't suppose there's anything here," the policeman said to himself, "but you can never tell."

Even when he had the information neatly written down in his notebook he was not sure if it was relevant or not.

"What it may mean, and what it does mean," he said to himself, "might be two different things."

However he was a careful man and in spite of aching feet and a sharp hunger he checked on what he had found.

Fortunately for his feet he was able to do most of his checking on the telephone.

"I reckon that does mean something," he told himself. He turned in his report and went home to have his supper. "Have you found the little girl?" his wife asked eagerly. "No," he said; he paused in his eating, considered whether to tell her what he had found, decided against it, and went back methodically to eating his meat pie.

So it came about that Superintendent Winter, still waiting with what patience he could muster, received the news that two tickets had been booked on the Victoria to Dover coach that night by someone in Pontifex Passage.

"They left a telephone number. An address or telephone number is always asked for apparently," said Coffin. "And this telephone number, Pompey 3189, proved to be the Booth house in Pontifex Passage."

"An empty house," grunted Winter. "Anyone could use it."

"And anyone did. The tickets were booked in the name of O'Finney. Nerve, you know."

"No, just the name on the murderer's mind. This murderer has nerves, not nerve."

"And the tickets are for an adult and a child."

"So I see. Stupid, really. So easy to get two tickets, so easy to give a false name and telephone number."

"I know," said Coffin. "This murderer is stupid and flustered: a nasty combination."

"And they were single tickets. No return envisaged. Doesn't that strike you?"

"All we have to do," said Coffin, trying to show a confidence he did not really feel, "is to get there this evening and wait for the coach to leave Victoria. If they are on it we shall get them."

"Yes. An hour and a half to go. I hope we won't be too late. I hope we are not already too late."

"Does it strike you as strongly as it does me that the other place to get to quickly is the Booth house? Right. I'm with you."

Before leaving, Winter sent off an order to the coach station requesting that the ten-thirty Dover coach should not leave until the police had given permission. He put down the receiver on protests and cries for explanation.

"I wish I could feel certain that we would get there in time," he worried. "How many men have you sent?"

"Two are there now. Two more will be on their way, and I have asked for a Flying Squad car to be placed at the departure gate. They are blocked. The ten-thirty coach cannot leave until we say so."

Mr. Booth's house, although it had received the light and passing attentions of Mrs. Daft, looked and smelt unlived-in.

"Not that it ever was what you would call a cosy home," said Coffin on whom Mr. Booth's establishment had a lowering effect.

They made a rapid tour of the house from top to bottom. It was quite empty, although their progress threw some interesting lights on Mr. Booth's housekeeping. (Why, for instance, did he have three dozen shaving mugs with pictures of Edward VII's coronation on them? Mr. Booth was not so old, impossible to believe he was even shaving then. "Generations of battiness there if you ask me," said Coffin.) It revealed the drawbacks of having Mrs. Daft to work for you. She had stored up sets and sets of half-worn gloves, handkerchiefs, stockings and even shoes, all plainly purloined property from her various employers. They were packed up in neat parcels and boxes, labelled 'Property of D. Daft and left by her for safe keeping', and placed on Mr. Booth's unused top floor. Several families of mice had made their peaceful homes in the middle of Mrs. Daft's trophies.

The two policemen descended to the hall. It was lit by a single electric bulb and contained a pile of circulars and a collection of milk bottles, some of which were empty, and some of which unluckily were only half empty. Coffin looked away quickly.

Winter was made of sterner material. He sniffed. "This last one's quite fresh."

"I don't fancy a cuppa here, if you do."

Winter pinched his lips and ignored the jest. "I'm going down to the kitchen."

"No one is here you know," said Coffin. "I'm too old a one at this game to be fooled. I'd be able to tell. There's no one here, not upstairs or downstairs or hidden in a cupboard."

"All the same, I'm going to the kitchen."

The kitchen was the most unused room in a desolate house, for it was never touched. Mr. Booth did any cooking he might want on a gas-ring in his bedroom where he brewed up milk and the glue he used for the few hats he still made with fine impartiality and indifference to smells.

In the kitchen Mrs. Daft had been content to let the dust of ages settle. There was a strong smell of old fish.

"No one is living here," said Winter, "but someone has been here all the same." He pointed to the door. The dust and rubbish which lay thickly on the floor had been swept back in a circular area by the door. "That door has been opened, recently and more than once."

By the door was a thick short stick. "That stick could have been used to kill Evelyn."

Coffin knew better than to touch it but he went over and inspected it. "Right enough. But if there are prints on it, we can't take too much notice of them. The murderer was in and out of the house don't forget."

"Get them all the same." Winter looked at his watch. "An hour to go."

At that moment in the empty house the telephone began to ring.

"Pompey 3189?"

"Yes," said Winter.

"I'm glad to tell you that the change of bookings from the ten-thirty coach from Victoria to Dover to the nine-thirty coach has been arranged. You can collect the seats at the booking office."

"Not an hour to go," said Winter putting down the receiver. "Not ten minutes."

CHAPTER FOURTEEN

ISOBEL MADE STRAIGHT for the house where she knew the murderer must be. It was not the Booth house, where unknown to her Winter and Coffin were standing in the hall, for she was better at guessing than the police.

"This is not a guess," she said to herself. "I know. Of course I know." She staggered a little as she ran and she wondered hastily if this was the result of too much wine and too many sleeping tablets.

She hurried, but the murderer was there before her.

She stopped at the right house, which was Christopher Cobley's house, and looked up at it. It seemed empty and lifeless, but this was what she had expected.

She walked round to the back, slipping on the autumn leaves lying on the path, and rang the bell.

No answer.

She rang again. Still no reply, but a sound.

This time she rang and banged on the door angrily. "You can come out. I know you are there."

It was possible that she herself was in some danger, but to this she was indifferent; she knew that Minny was in danger—in danger of fear and anguish if not of pain and death, and she knew there might be this too.

"Hurry up," she shouted, still banging.

The back door opened slowly, it opened only a few inches, then stopped, it was on a chain.

The face Isobel was waiting to see looked out at her through a crack. To her surprise the face looked as she had always known it—good-natured, gentle and half smiling. There was no sign of the complex emotions of fear, suspicion and hate which must be hidden there, nor of the love which she knew was there too. Isobel understood about the love which was so deep and passionate that it had caused two murders. She had reason to understand.

"You know why I've come. I've come to get Minny. Let me have Minny."

"I've no idea what you are talking about. Go away. You're mad." The door began to close.

But Isobel had her foot in the door and she was full of strength.

"You know all right. Oh, and I know too that you killed those men. And I know you have Minny here now. Minny, Minny," called Isobel hoping for an answering voice.

"Go away, you lying, accusing bitch." The voice shook. "I hate you. Clear off."

"Yes, I know you are angry. I can understand that." Isobel forced her voice to be calm.

"Angry? I'm not angry. I've got a sense of justice that's all. I wanted to be treated like a human being. I am one, aren't I? I feel helpless. People like me are caught in a machine."

Isobel laughed.

"And people like you laugh. That's exactly like you. Can you wonder that I'm resentful? Did you think I was going to lie down like a doormat for ever? Just because in my way I loved you all?"

"You've never spoken like this before." Isobel gathered her strength together. "But you do me an injustice. I meant to be good to you."

"You hardly noticed I was there."

"This has nothing to do with Minny." Isobel spoke sternly.

"It has *now*. An eye for an eye. One daughter is as good as another."

Isobel was very white. "How did you get Minny here?"

There was a laugh. "Oh, she *came*. I can manage her. I said to her several times before she went away: if you can get away from Granny's, come back to *me*; it's the best thing you can do for your mother. So she came because she thought she was helping you. It was a clever idea of mine. Oh, I provided the opportunity by telephoning."

Isobel drew in her breath.

"Of course it never struck me that Gran would put her in a taxi instead of a bus, but fortunately Minny is frightened of taxis because of what I had told her of Men. (I must tell you more about that some time.) And she knew all about buses and tubes because we'd had many little trips together that *you* knew nothing about."

"So that was where she got the tube ticket."

"Well, you never took the child out did you? Get on a number eleven bus I said and trust me to meet it. And I did. My luck held. If you can call it luck."

"You're mad."

"Oh, I knew you'd say that."

Once more an attempt was made to close the door, but Isobel's foot was firmly planted. She looked at the chain with a speculative eye.

"You won't get round *that*," said the murderer with satisfaction.

"You *are* mad," said Isobel.

"I'm not mad. I know myself. Mad people never do, do they? Well, do they? Oh, don't answer." The voice dropped. "I wasn't wanted. People like me are never wanted."

"That's always the delusion," murmured Isobel.

"Delusion. Was it delusion that the child died?"

"Do you think I haven't met this sort of thing before?" said Isobel, half in pity.

"Oh, I was a fool," said the murderer bitterly. "I see that now. But I've got to protect myself."

"This has nothing to do with Minny," said Isobel, putting a weight on each syllable.

"One daughter is as good as another."

The repetition of this phrase frightened Isobel.

"But I'm not frightened of you, don't think I am. You won't give me away."

"You're wrong."

"Oh, I'm wrong? Well, why are you still here then? Why haven't you run off shrieking and shouting long before this? I'm safe with you. I liked you, you see, admired you, that gives me a hold over you. You won't let *me* go easily."

"Nonsense you are talking." Isobel made another attempt to push the door.

The murderer laughed. "You see, not even trying. You don't really want me to get caught."

"Give Minny to me and I don't care what you do. Run away, drown yourself."

"A good idea. But I shan't go alone."

The night was closing in round the two figures as the moon dropped in the sky and the mist came up again.

Isobel rattled the door in mounting anger. "I'm going for the police," and she turned.

"Wait a minute. You wouldn't really go for the police would you? Not for me?"

Isobel did not answer.

Now the ascendancy was passing to her and she began to understand that the force and energy which had seemed inexhaustible in the murderer were nearly at an end. If she held on now she would win.

"You wouldn't?"

Isobel still did not answer.

"Yes, I see you would," said the murderer who had been studying her face. "All right then, let's see who's quickest on their feet. I have made my plans."

The door was slammed in Isobel's face.

She stood there for a moment puzzled and undecided. Then she ran back round the path, falling down in the darkness. She was already too late.

Two figures were hurrying in the misty gloom through Pontifex Passage.

"Why aren't there any policemen here," she cried. "Minny, Minny," she called but the wind which was rising and carrying away the mist also carried away her voice.

"Minny, Minny," she called, beginning to run. But Minny never looked back.

CHAPTER FIFTEEN

THE POLICE CAR headed into the crowded road.

"It ought to be easy enough to stop the coach," said Winter with an assurance he did not feel. "We can't be sure she's on it. We got the message after all."

"She'd take a chance on seats being free. We know what she's capable of."

"Or rather, unluckily, we don't."

"That's a risk we've got to take."

"You and I know," said Winter, "exactly who we expect to see at the coach station. Proof, however, unless we can shake a confession, is something else."

"Maybe we shall do exactly that."

"We hope," said Winter. He looked at the traffic, and then at his watch. "I'm thinking that this is going to be one of the cases where we get the murderer first and our case afterwards."

"Not a bad way of doing it." Coffin was studying the traffic too. "I'll be satisfied if we get hold of the child Minny." He wiped away the mist on the window. "Can't this go any faster?"

"What put me on the right road was two pieces of conversation. The first came from the barmaid and it showed that the constable Evelyn had practically told the murderer that *he* knew. A silly, risky thing to do, and he paid for it."

Coffin nodded, he was still looking out of the window.

"The other piece of conversation was more important: it was a complete give-away on the part of the murderer. I mean, of course, what the other young constable had to tell us."

"About the clothes?"

"Yes, the murderer knew that Evelyn was killed in plain clothes." Winter went on, "It was after that I began to see the significance of evidence which had, of course, worried me all along. Jack O'Finney had had his hair cut, and he had been tied up when he died. I saw that these two facts were related to each other and to the murderer."

"I see now," said Coffin almost absently. "The murderer cut his hair." His fingers were drumming impatiently on his knees.

"The two concrete scraps of evidence we have are the bloodstained child's handkerchief and the child's clothes. Both had been in possession of the murderer. Remember it was on a Monday O'Finney was killed. Washday."

"I suppose the child found her handkerchief. . . . Funny how I thought it might be Mrs. Duveen."

"Her sort don't kill. She wouldn't put herself in the way of wearing a prison dress and waiting for the rope. She has feeling but it runs out pretty thin. We had to look for someone with real hearty human feelings. Evelyn knew that, poor chap. And I suppose he knew, being a local boy, what was likely to be the motive."

"Mad, poor thing," said Coffin. "We're pretty close to the coach station now."

"She wanted revenge. And revenge for something that never really happened. Six months ago Dr. O'Finney delivered a baby girl at St. Clare's. The irony of it is that he only took the case on as a special favour, the mother was a senseless sort of girl who had thoroughly neglected herself, which was stupid as she was one of these rare blood cases. As a result the baby never lived —not a case of being born and then dying—it never breathed at all. The mother cared very little, and was in any case, poor thing, shortly to suffer a fairly common sort of post-childbirth insanity. But the grandmother took the whole thing very badly. Perhaps it was the double tragedy, but she began to declare that the baby had been murdered because Dr. O'Finney thought people like her and her daughter should not be allowed to have children."

"I dare say he did talk some sort of mad eugenics," said Coffin. "But the child Minny?"

"That I can't altogether explain," said Winter uneasily. "Part of her general craziness, I suppose."

"There's the coach," shouted Coffin.

The police car had turned into the coach station just as the coach, with Mrs. Daft and Minny sitting side by side, drew out.

Winter was leaning out of the car shouting directions but when the coach was driven into the kerb by a perturbed and puzzled driver it was Coffin who was on the step and inside before Mrs. Daft could act.

"Now you don't want to do anything silly, lady," he said, gently grasping her moving hands.

He looked down at the bottle. "That's nasty stuff, lady."

"It was for me, not the child," said Mrs. Daft, her face puckering.

There was no more fierceness left in her. She collapsed completely as soon as she was alone with the policemen. Minny had been sent home to her parents.

"I didn't mean any harm to the little love," sobbed Mrs. Daft. "I started all that story about The Man in the first place to get them all sent away. I knew all this was going to happen and I wanted them out of it. There never was any man, I made it all up and told Minny that it was to help her mother. I let her think that everything that happened afterwards was to help her mother. She loves her mother. I loved them all too once but after I lost my granddaughter and my daughter I could see that they thought people like me were just a joke and that it didn't matter if we were killed. So then I knew I had to show them." She was crying. "But I was wrong to make use of Minny, I was wicked, I see I was wicked."

No further questions were possible.

Perdita and Tom were happy, gay and young again. Berry and Fanny were happy too. Only Poldy was a little gloomy. "Both of you going to leave me, I see," he said. "Oh, well I shall keep your jobs open. Marriages don't always last."

"Ours will," said Fanny, speaking for them all.

Robert and Isobel faced each other with apologies.

"She won't want to come near me," Robert had said to his mother-in-law. He stared gloomily at his reflection in the mirror above the rosewood table. It was an old mirror and his reflection wobbled back at him.

"Don't worry about Isobel. I'll bring her up to scratch."

Brought up to scratch by Lady Passey, Isobel now faced her husband unhappily.

"I'm very ashamed of myself, Robert. Minny, Mrs. Daft, everything, I don't show up in a very good light, do I?"

"None of us do. Don't think I'm very proud of myself."

"And on top of everything else I behaved unspeakably to that unlucky Christopher just because he was frightened."

"I was frightened myself."

"So was I," admitted Isobel and she held out her hand.

"And you know the one thing that is worrying Minny more than anything?" she asked several minutes later

"No."

"That she threw away her pink gloves because she didn't want me to know she'd taken money from Mrs. Daft. The money was in the glove."

Robert laughed. "How like my daughter to throw out the baby with the bath water. She could have kept the gloves. I'll give her six more pairs."

"Say a dozen," said Isobel. They both began to laugh.

"And the poor little baby was not killed by Jack

O'Finney," said Coffin. "The hospital had plenty of witnesses. So the whole terrible business was rooted in a mistake."

"Yes," said Winter a trifle sadly. "I suppose you could say that is true of all murders in a sense. They are all of them always rooted in a mistake."

If you have enjoyed this book, you might wish to join the Walker British Mystery Society.

For information, please send a postcard or letter to:

Paperback Mystery Editor

**Walker & Company
720 Fifth Avenue
New York, NY 10019**